Free Doug

A Novel

J.P. McMurphy

"Climb the mountains and get their good tidings. Nature's peace will flow into you as sunshine flows into trees. The winds will blow their own freshness into you, and the storms their energy, while cares will drop off like autumn leaves."

-John Muir

The first thing I remember is the smell of flowers. My eyelids slowly cracked open, a sharp beam of light seeping through the blinds stung my eyes. My neck felt like it had been *welded* in place as I attempted to pan the small room. I tried to pry back my memory for anything, it was empty. The bed I was in tilted up at the waist, railings on either side. A hospital bed. An iv in my right arm. I lay for ten minutes, trying to pull anything from my blank memory. Peering through the gap between the blinds and window frame, I was able to make out snow-capped mountains on the foggy horizon.

My body was a thin, empty shell of skin and bones. I attempted to bend my leg, my knee was locked in place. Two vases filled with sad, wilted flowers sat on the bedside table.

6 months earlier...

      I sat on the hot pavement near the ice-cooler, waiting for Doug. I had no idea what Doug looked like, no idea what he was driving. I did know Doug was, at this point, nearly 11 hours late because he had hurt his back 'loading a bed'. I was *baking* in the California sun. Peak season wildfire smoke so thick I could barely see the pumps.

      Out of the haze rolled a late 70's, once upon a time white, rusted out cargo van with no doors, no bumpers, no muffler, mirrors that had been duck-taped back on and spare tires on all four wheels, into the station on two wheels. It came screeching to a stop across three parking spots. As it flew by the front doors, I could faintly see the outline of a trailer dragging behind it but it was hard to tell what was on it with all the smoke from the van. When the smoke finally cleared I could see there was only one item on that trailer. A torn, tattered, piss-stained bed. I picked up my backpack, started hesitantly making my way towards the van. As I approached the driver's side, a bean bag of a man maybe 75 going on some age that never was, wearing an oil stained, *severely* battered Stetson, a tattered, stretched out t-shirt and a pair of shorts likely from last century, who looked like life had been beating the *ancient fuck* out of him for most of those years, had the hood popped and was dumping in oil, sloshing, spilling all over the sizzling engine...

      "Doug?"

6 months, two weeks earlier...

      I hiked towards the smoky blue sky, battling for each step now. The relentless *white* sun *baking* me *alive*. According to the maps I'd printed off at the San Francisco Public Library, I was up around 12,000 feet now. *The High*

Sierra. According to the tally marks I'd been making on my tattered map, nearly two weeks had passed since I'd departed the last re-supply opportunity. I was *cremated.* I was out of food. Halfway up the steep, rocky, sun scorched slope, a wave of dizziness rushed over me. My arms and legs became heavy, I fell to my knees, threw up, and again. Then came the tightness in my chest, as if a hand was squeezing my heart, trying to pop it like a water balloon. *The wheels had finally fallen off.* I sat, leaned against a boulder, lit up a joint.

New York City

7 months earlier...

 As we joined the landing pattern for Laguardia, I peered out the glinting oval through patches of gray, wispy clouds. I noticed a massive cemetery below us. Headstones packed in like sardines upon the green hills of the city, acre upon acre. The past. Some had left a larger mark on the sands of time than others. Most of those headstones had been in the ground longer than I had been alive. I was ready for whatever life and fate chose to hurl at me next. I was ready to go *anytime*.

 After landing at Laguardia, I got lost in the maze of the subway for several hours. Hopping on trains, hopping off onto platforms. Staring at signs that appeared to be breathing. I was out on Roosevelt Ave, striding under the shadow of the elevated train, its trestles and piers, rivets, and graffiti. The sound of generators. Pig's heads, brains, intestines. Trucks selling glass pipes, Spanish Romances, jeans, supersonic glasses, cell phones, paintings, vinyl records, yo-yo's, chopsticks. It smelled like fried chicken and french fries, sweet fried plantations, and grilled corn. The horns were honking, and a small ugly car gunned around the others. Boxing gloves with the Puerto Rican flag hung from the rearview mirror. The bars came every doorway and they were dark. Loud music was playing, but if you looked inside, a table covered in an Olympic number of beer bottles. It was the scene of migrants getting plastered.

Eventually I found my way to Central Park, called Truman. He lived west of the park. No Answer. It was a steamy July day in the city, Central Park was a painting that had come to life. A pickup game of basketball on the half court in the shade of an old oak. A mom holding her toddler up to drink from a fountain. A girl throwing a frisbee for her golden. The pond sparkled in the mid-day sun. Ducks splashed and fluttered. Shorebirds floated on tufts of wind. People filled the lawn, laying on blankets, reading, soaking up the sun. An hour passed, my phone lit up.

"Sorry phone died. 72nd and Broadway."

I walked south for ten blocks then west towards the Hudson. Twenty minutes later, there he was standing on the corner lighting up a dart. Smoke ribbons swirled in the soft afternoon light. George sat next to him on the sidewalk. Truman had rescued George from the shelter. Big City George we called him, a shin-high white Scotty with an under-bite that put a permanent grin on his face. George spotted me first, frantically pulling Truman in the direction I was approaching from.

Truman was like a brother to me. We had been on the same peewee hockey team, friends ever since. A Minnesotan through and through. King of the turn-around slap shot. Hockey and skiing in the winter, golf in the summer, hunting in the fall, fishing year round. Built like a lumberjack. Could have played Paul Bunyon with almost no costume. He found himself living in Manhattan the last 7 years because he had landed a job on Broadway when he was 22 and his booming voice had been a staple on the scene ever since. George led the way to the apartment ten stories above the street. I lit a joint. Before long the smoke was so thick I couldn't see George across the room. We opened windows and through the laughter tried to fan smoke out but it was no use. The late afternoon sunlight gushed through the tall buildings illuminating the haze into a mango glow. Truman realized it was time to head towards the theater for the evening show.

We dipped down into the subway, hopped on the 1 train rolling towards Times Square, popped up onto the street from the soupy subway. The streets were awash with people coming off the buses, coming out of the subway station with every roar of the train coming in, welling up onto the streets in waves.

We stopped off at a small pub called Beer Culture. Forty-eight minutes until showtime. We sat at the bar. Truman ordered an *Edmunds Oast*. I ordered a Volvik. Four minutes later it was time for the *Egregious Cosmonaut* with a shot of bourbon. A quick glance at his watch, 44 minutes until showtime. Four minutes later it was time for the *Coldsmoke* washed down by another shot of bourbon. I guzzled a Saratoga. 35 minutes until showtime. We walked out the door, crossed the street, began walking east towards the bright lights of Broadway, the stage Half jogging now, weaving through the crowd. Into the colorful flashing lights and noise, buildings touching the sky. Weaving, dodging, running through the crowd.

"I gotta go pooooootty!" Truman belted out in perfect pitch as we stream past dazed tourists through the heart of Times Square. Dancing through the crowd now. "I gottaaaa gooo POOTTTTTTTYYYYYY!!" Truman bellowed laced with rich vibrato. A block east of Times Square we duck into an alley, stop outside a door with a security code box on it. Truman enters a code, we enter a sea of curtains. After pushing through several layers of curtains we walk out onto the *stage* of the 105 year old Lyceum theater. The oldest continuously running theater in New York City. Landmark status. Thirty two minutes until showtime. The seats are empty except for a few ushers. The air was charged with energy. Something was about to happen here.

The show was *On the 20th Century* starring Kristen Chenoweth and Peter Gallagher. Truman had snagged me a seat within spitting range of the stage. It was a comic opera, set on a luxury train in the 1920's traveling from Chicago to New York. Chenowith played Lily, a crazy Hollywood actress and Gallagher played Oscar, a bankrupt theater producer trying desperately to convince Lily to star in his next big currently unwritten hit.

After the show I made my way to the backstage line. A small crowd hovered around the door guarded by Arthur, the usher. I lingered behind everyone. Truman emerged in the doorway "Yo Jack!" I walked past the line, past Arthur, through the doorway, down narrow black stairs, into the world of backstage Broadway. As usual, the real show was backstage. We walked through tight corridors between piles of equipment and props. In the center of the widest corridor several members of the cast huddled around a large bowl of punch with gin and melted-ice. The after-party had begun. I found a spot along the edge behind some of the stage techs and watched as one after another, whoever had a bit or a song or dance took to the open area next to the punch bowl and entertained the room. After an hour we walked out the back door of the theater where a large crowd had gathered waiting for autographs.

We decided to hop on the subway, head towards Brooklyn. Manchini lived out there. We decided to visit Manchini. We found the nearest subway station, dropped down underneath the city and hopped on the 7 train rumbling towards Brooklyn. The hot dank subway was crawling with people. From the doped up homeless to finely dressed Wall Streeters', Broadway stars and everything in between. It was very crowded, standing room only. We were sharing the middle pole with a lady and her daughter. A beautiful black woman, dressed to the nines. We swayed in silence as the train rolls down the tracks. Suddenly she looks at Truman with a smile. "I recognize you... YES! We went to your play last night. You were gooood!"

Love was cool as pie, hip from head to toe. She had grown up in the Haight Ashbury district of San Francisco, in the middle of it all. A hippie turned private school administrator, out for a week to see a few shows with her daughter.

We arrived at our stop in Brooklyn, which just so happened to be Love and her daughters stop as well.

"If either of you ever make it to San Francisco you've got a place to stay!"

"I'm going to be in San Francisco in three days, I bought a multi-city airline ticket and that's my next stop." I said in semi-disbelief.

As we walked in separate directions my phone lit up, "this is LOVE." It was one of those eerily impossible coincidences where the 'universe' seems to be telling you something, what, I had no idea.

After walking through the muggy mid-summer evening for ten minutes, we found Manchini's building. An old warehouse remodeled into rugged apartments. Manchini was arriving home from his deliveries for an underground cannabis bike delivery service. We sat in wicker lounge chairs at the glass topped table on the patio. Manchini began to pack and pass a bong around. At the end of every shift they received a free bag. After nearly two hours of continuous puffing, we finished the entire bag. Nearly comatose, I asked Manchini if I could ride a delivery shift for him. Fully comatose, he bet me the free eighth plus another half ounce I wouldn't survive it. Riding through the boroughs at night, no clue where I'm going. Not the foggiest idea where the deliveries would take me. What could possibly go wrong out there? There was only one way to find out.

I walked down the West Side riverfront along the Hudson from 72nd all the way to Pier 1 on the southwest tip of Manhattan. It was another hot humid day in the city, a warm summer wind blew in off the river. The heat seamed to radiate from all surfaces, all directions. As I walked down the waterfront I came across a rollerblader trick skating through a line of cones. He was whipping through the cones with crossovers, slalom, dance like movements. After each intricate pass he would make large loops to either side of the cones. He wore large earmuff headphones and *clearly* was in his own world. A small fluctuating crowd gathered around. Some darted in and dropped money into the upturned cowboy hat that lay on the ground. The Hudson sparkled in the late afternoon sun, Lady Liberty framed the roller artist with her torch. After my tenth bowl things began to get *hazy*.

Truman was busy with two shows today. I decided tonight would be a good night to start my cannabis delivery career. I grabbed a coffee and a slice of pie at a small cafe, hopped on a train rolling towards Brooklyn and before long was in front of Manchini's. He had already picked up the deliveries from the 'headquarters', all I had to do was deliver them. There were five deliveries tonight. Manchini handed me a map of New York City, wished me luck. He looked nervous for me. I was too high to be much of anything else. I hopped on his red nova one speed with red tires. I lit a joint, went out into the quiet summer night and started hiking down Franklin Avenue, until the small American houses gave way to the ghetto buildings and then the huge Cathedral of Chinatown, over the hill thru the dark trees and down the long block that extended out to the freeway like a jetty.

The first delivery was in Queens and had a star next to it with the word *priority. Not long after I started biking a dog began chasing me. A massive, gnarly looking Doberman mix. He was barking furiously, biting at my ankles. I ripped down an alley trying to lose him. We zoomed past a junkie nodding off beside a garbage can, the dog attacked him like he had been dipped in beef broth. He regained a marginal level of consciousness as the dog shook him like a chew toy, ripped his coat off, and ran back towards the main road. The man tipped over onto his side and drifted back into the land of the poppy. I hung a left on the next side street, crossed over a small bridge, into a park. Hobos roamed like zombies waltzing between the trees.

I hopped on the G, then transferred to the 7 at Court Square. We swooped up and down over the bridge into flushing Chinatown, broke out the other side into the dusky glow of east flushing. The ghetto buildings tagged in Spanish, the decaying houses of the Irish.

The door swung open. In the doorway stood a man. He looked like a soldier. The haircut, build, to go along with the pain in his eyes. Beside him stood a short, petite, Asian woman wearing a flowing silk robe with Chinese characters on it. She was smiling and I could see her nipples poking against the thin silk of the robe. He was taking a large drag off his cigarette as he squinted at me. The room was stonework, with a three tiered antique fountain in the center. Lights illuminated the sparkling water, spouts of water splashed continuously. An Asian man dressed in a blue and white robe walked into the room from an oval doorway on the other side of the fountain. BANG!! BANG!! Two deafening gunshot-esque sounds echoed violently around the room. I hit the deck. The woman and soldier were still standing, smoking, seemingly unconcerned. My eyes went back to the old man. He was lighting a firework held between his fingers. He watched the wick burn down and at the last possible second, calmly lobbed the firework into the air above the fountain. BANG!! I flinched again and covered my ears as the deafening sound reverberated between the stone walls. *Fuck Me.* I heard the hiss of another fuse. BANG!! The man in the robe started casually strolling around the fountain, lighting another. I was the only person in the room that seemed startled or bothered by the fireworks. BANG! BANG!

The woman was walking towards the fountain. She undid the belt of the robe, let it fall onto the ground, completely naked under the robe. She dipped a toe into the water, then slipped into the water and began floating on her back, along with several exploded fireworks, letting the water arches plash in her mouth. *How high was I?* I held out the bag of cannabis towards the soldier as he handed me a few 20's. BANG! BANG! I turned and ran for the door. Outside, the skyline of Midtown Manhattan sat dark against the hazy blue dusk.

The next delivery was a Brooklyn address, the Greenwood Heights neighborhood. I rode the 7 southwest, hopped on the G, and rolled into Brooklyn. As I smoked a joint in a park I pulled out my map, I was close. I biked down the block, around the corner, pulled up to a rowhouse with the shades shut. The dark red paint was cracked like dried mud. I pulled out the order, a half o of *sour D* and a quarter of *OG kush*. As I knocked on the front door, I got the sense this wasn't the safest part of town by the charred frame of a car out front smoldering with dancing coals. That, and the steel bars on the windows. The door swung open wildly. In the doorway stood a giant bald man wearing a black dress and steel-toed construction boots. He was at least 6'5" and built like a *brick shit-house.* The dress he was wearing was not made for someone with that type of build. It was so tight, at first glance it looked like it was *painted* on. He did have painted on eyebrows to go with his real mustache. His eyes were shaded in a way similar to a dalmatians. He wore a giant mahogany colored lip stick stained smile. It was an original look. *The drag clown.* He invited me in and introduced himself as Keith. In the middle of the living room to my right I noticed a mechanical bucking bronc. *How high was I?* The lighting was dim, a small disco ball twirled slowly from the ceiling above the horse. The walls were painted multiple colors and had many large holes in them. The room had four giant speakers, one in each corner. "Gotta get high as faaaaaack 'fore I ride Alan, my horse." Keith said in a voice that sounded like he had inhaled helium.

"We've got you taken care of here."

He handed me the cash. I handed him the cannabis.

"Wanna get high 'fore you roll?" Keith asked.

"Sure."

He walked over, grabbed the bong from Alan's saddle bag, packed it, handed it to me. As I was taking my first rip the sound system sprang to life. Salsa music began blaring at a volume level that was loud enough to swim in. After we had cashed the bong, Keith walked over to the horse, pulled the sombrero off Alan's head, placed it on his. He began stretching, balancing on one leg as he pulled the other leg completely behind him. His eyes were closed. When he was finished stretching, he knelt and said a prayer. Then Keith was in the saddle. He pulled on the weightlifting gloves that were hanging from the horse's ears. Next, he produced a pre-rolled joint from somewhere in the abyss of his dress. He lit it. "Ok, over on the wall is the button to turn this rig on. Once you hit that button, I have ten seconds 'fore ol' Alan here tries to buck me into the East River." "Ok." I walked over and pushed the button. Keith looked extremely anxious for what was about to happen. He was staring at the back of Alan's head, puffing the joint to smithereens. I heard a loud high pitched sound, like the whine of a jet engine. The horse jerked a little as if waking up. "IF SHIT HITS THE FAN PUSH THAT RED BUTTON ON THE WALL!" Keith yelled over the noise as Alan sprang to life and started whirling him around like a god damn rag doll. The mechanical horse rose and fell from the ground with the speed, power and rhythm of a piston on a coal powered locomotive. Nothing was stopping Alan. Keith hung on for dear life. The look on his face was somewhere between panic and sheer joy. Up and down, around and around and around they went. "Riiiiiiiiiddddddddeeeee Emmmmm!!!!" He yelled as the horse steadily picked up speed until he was writhing so violently I was getting ready to dodge Keith, if he was thrown off with this sort of velocity he was going to hit wall before he hit ground. I had no idea how he was staying on the maniacally bucking machine.

Finally, Keith lost his grip on the handlebars coming out the sides of Alan's head and was launched into the wall, leaving a massive crater in the sheetrock. The horse picked up speed without Keith on its back. I walked over, pushed the red button. Alan halted. I walked around to the other side of the room, Keith was in the fetal position amongst a pile of sheet-rock.

"You ok Keith?"

"Balls." he squeaked as he gingerly rocked back and forth.

"Enjoy that weed bud..." I walked towards the door, out of the wall shaking Salsa music.

The next address was on the Upper West Side. I lit a bowl, ripped it down and blazed through the haze, hopped on the F train back towards Manhattan, transferred to the C at Washington Square Park, hopped off at Columbus Circle in the southwest corner of Central Park. I biked into the Park, found a group of trees, smoked a joint. I blazed up the West Side of the park, then turned west towards the river, over curbs, down alley's, through patches of grass. No clue where I was going. After 45 minutes of biking in what seemed like circles, I stopped at a convenience store and asked if I was close to the address I was looking for. (I was a late hold-out to join the smart phone 'revolution' and unless I was delivering weed in unknown parts of New York City, in the dark, it was easy enough to get by). The man behind the counter looked like he was *hippy-flipping*. He pointed to the map and explained the directions with what seemed to be a fairly high level of confidence, then as he was almost done, he says. "Waaaaiiiittt a minute, it's upsiiiidee dooowwwwn!" He flipped the map around, pointed to the same portion of the map on the opposite side. "Errrrrr waaaiiiiiittt...how many maps we got here?" I soon realized he was so far from this planet, deciphering the map was not possible. I walked outside, noticed an old woman ripping a dart alongside the ice-cooler. I walked over and said hi, asked her how to get to the address. She smiled, took a long draw on her dart. "Around the corner, you were close."

It was a grand, old building. I told the doorman guarding the front door I had a delivery for 1b. He checked his notepad, waved me through. I walked through the marble floored entry way, pushed the button for the gold trimmed elevator. As I waited, the old woman from the gas station walked through the lobby and stood beside me.

"You live here?"

She was smiling. "How do you think I knew where it was? I needed to grab darts. Long night of writing ahead of me. I'm assuming you have my other ingredient....?"

"If a quarter of *grape alien* is what you're looking for, yes ma'am, I do."

We made it to the door of her apartment, she invited me in. It was a very nice place. Manhattan jazz played on the record player. Antique furniture and lamps graced the living room. The whole place was meticulously decorated with expensive art and the kind of decor I imagine you find in 5th Avenue shops.

"So you're a writer eh?" I asked.

"Yes I am, trying to wrap up this damn novel, burning it on both ends if you know what I'm saying," she said with another big smile.

She was a short woman, maybe 5'2", with thick white hair, quite old, 70's, dressed in fine, fashionable clothing. Everything about her radiated *class*. Her eyes were a deep blue and filled with kindness and ageless beauty. Despite her small frail frame she had a toughness about her in the way she moved and spoke. I pulled out the jar of *grape alien* and put it on the counter. She picked it up and rotated the jar as she closely inspected the product. "Dank." she said as she handed me a wad of cash.

"Wanna get torched?" she asked.

"Yes ma'am."

She pulled out a black rolling tray with rounded corners. On it was a lighter, rolling papers and a metal grinder. She went to work rolling up a joint. Her long skinny fingers worked with precision and grace. She fired it up and sucked in a long hard draw like she had been waiting for it all day. She passed it to me, I took a few puffs, passed it back to her.

"I'm Jack."

"Effie, nice to meet you Jack" she said as she exhaled an enormous puff of smoke.

"Nice to meet you Effie. Have you written other books?"

"Oh, I've written a few."

She smiled, continued to take rips like a sailor. After we had finished the joint she walked into the living room and sat down at her typewriter. Around the typewriter sat a bottle of coke resting in a bucket of ice with a clean tumbler beside it, a plate of cookies, a mug of milk also on ice. She set down the rolling tray along with the fresh bag of bud beside it.

"So you're going to write all night?"

"Depends on the night. On a good night, I get rolling, lose track of time, before I know it it's 4-5 in the morning. I've got a month to wrap this damn thing up, get it just the way I want it. It's never enough time." She pulled a *fronto leaf* from the top pocket of her blouse and went to work rolling a blunt that could have stopped a small army.

"Gotta get the night started right eh there Jack?" she said with a wink.

"I like your style Effie, hope that book comes together nicely for you," I said as I walked out of the apartment through the lobby, into the sticky summer evening.

The next address was in Harlem. The name on the delivery list simply said D. Davinci. Beside the name was a note, *'will try to haggle...also, NOT living on this planet!'* I found my way to Harlem, then quickly became disoriented in relation to the map. I stopped and lit a joint, figured if this character wasn't living on this planet, I had best not be anywhere near it either. Soon after I finished the joint, it became clear where on the map I was headed. It wasn't far, 3 blocks north, 2 blocks east.

The condition of the surrounding houses and apartments declined shockingly fast in those 5 blocks. I had seemingly walked into a quasi-war zone. I found a building that matched Davinci's address and hesitantly walked towards it despite fielding many looks letting me know that I was in fact not even close to where I was supposed to be. Two towering men of quite possibly eastern European descent approached quickly from the lawn and blocked my path towards the front doors.

"We pound to dust and sell on streetcorner!"

"Ummm, nnnnot necessary guys...I have a delivery for a Mr. Davinci." I stammered.

"Dan!?" they both exclaimed wide eyed as if that was the key to the city. Why you not tell us, silly boy! They both put their arms around my shoulders and proudly escorted me to the front of the building.

"Through doors elevator to 37th floor third door on right!"

"You guys know him?" They both looked at each other, smiled, then back at me.

"Dan hovers above earth on blue cloud! Dan magic man!"

I forged on, into the lobby, beginning to wonder what in the lively fuck I was getting myself into here. In the lobby was a 'front desk' stripped of everything but its frame. A few remnants of no doubt once upon a time cupboards behind it. Apparently they had gone paperless. I looked to my right and located the elevator down the hall, walked towards it, joining the small crowd waiting for it to arrive. I counted at least 4 languages being spoken in the group, none of which I was able to speak or understand. The elevator on the right soon opened and a wall of people toppled into the hallway.

When the elevator car was clear, the small mob I was a part of began piling in. A steady stream of folks continued to join the waiting line. All sizes of people continued to pack into the creaking car, now sagging below floor level. Finally, the heavy door slowly slid shut, cutting off the flow of bodies and somehow, closed. It smelled like an armpit fried in a pan. I was pinned against the wall in the far back corner by a massive woman wearing a crop top that was cut one roll too high and yoga pants that were at least two sizes too small, so tight, I could scarcely suck in a breath. As soon as the doors where shut, numbers were called out in multiple languages.

Thankfully, the guy in closest proximity to the number board, appeared to speak all of them. I yelled thirty seven, and when nothing was added to the board of numbers, I took my best stab in Spanish, butchering it horribly no doubt. I'd hardly gotten it out of my mouth before another button was pushed and stop added to the nearly dozen selected buttons. On several floors someone in the back of the elevator car would need to get out. The folks in front toppled into the hallway, racing the door back into the stuffed car each time. It looked like a drill that had been practiced thousands of times. I was checked against the far wall each time by the wave of people scrambling back into the car. By the time I arrived at the thirty seventh floor I was choking on the putrid air and felt like I'd just lost a 10 round bout.

By this point there were 3 of us left on board. I stumbled out into the narrow, dark hallway and soon found apartment 37. I knocked twice, stepped back a few steps feeling a bit like I'd just lit the fuse of a bomb. There was a blue glow coming from under the door. Steps approached the door, then I heard a strange voice with a thick accent yell,"Who Der!?" in a high pitched mangy tone. "I've got a delivery here for Davinci." The deadbolt unlatched and the door swung open wildly revealing a short, frail, other worldly looking man standing awash in blue light. It seemed every light bulb in the small apartment had been changed to a bright blue bulb.

"Looking for Davinci??"

"Yes I am, did you order cannabis?"

He closed his eyes, after a long pause, opened them, looked at me, "I did."

"Looks like I've got 1 eighth for you here, *blueberry tahoe*"

His face lit up "Ooooooo, da bluuuuuue!"

"Yes, ok, it will be 50$ dollars please."

"Come on in my boy..."

I followed him into the blue haze of light. The apartment had one room with a small bathroom near the door, the ceiling was 16 ft high and the walls were covered from top to bottom with paintings. Colorful fantastical scenes all involving spaceships, UFO's, planets and blue light. One corner of the room was heaped with *heavily* used art supplies and a wall of paint cans. The middle of the room was taken up by an enormous spaceship sculpture made out of plaster or clay. The sheer weight of it looked to be causing the middle of the room to sag down. Inserted into the clay material were lights, mainly but not entirely blue, they were all flashing.

"You like ship?" asked Davinci.

"I do."

"Not done, ran into problems, building management said ship getting too big, could fall through floor...and if goes through floor, might go through all 36... so they make me put on 'hold' which not stop me, financial problems though, did."

I could see now how the entire room was sagging under the weight of the spaceship, the floor creaked loudly when I stepped towards it, I stepped back.

"You need art? I sell direct, NO consignments! NO contracts! Low! I need money!" Dan said loudly.

"These are some amazing pieces you have here Davinci."

"Call me Dan, no Davinci, call me Davinci."

"Nice to meet you Davinci."

Dan did a small twirl with outstretched arms presenting the wall of art to me.

"My art is unique art...unique mind, unique art...I do different!"

"That's an interesting accent you've got there Davinci, where are you from?"

He looked towards the ground, began talking in a soft tone.

"Romania where I born, parents sell me for 100 pound as baby, life very bad. Ceausescu regime, evil, evil, man. So I swim Danube to Yugoslovia to escape dumb bastard! Then I take ship to Lady Liberty. I live in this apartment for 22 years now, American dream!"

"Amazing...living completely off your art?"

"All I can do, that and swim, I damn good at swim...too old for dat *shiiiit* now."

"Isn't swimming the Danube considered nearly impossible?"

"Friend that swim with me not make it...I have *blue light*, nothing stop *blue light* baby!"

"Fuck yeah Davinci, where do you sell your art?"

"Outsider art fair. Outside it. They try to make do contracts, consignment! I tell no! Only cash! NO CONSIGNMENTS! I need to SURVIVE! So I sell outside. No problem."

"Isn't that thing in mid-January?"

"No one said being artist easy life! Terrible life! Art is all I have. I use art to go to different dimension, to forget my life."

"I'll tell you what Davinci, that bag is on the house tonight my friend."

"Da Bluuuuueeeee!!!!!?" He sang in a howl of excitement, then started doing some strange dance steps that vaguely resembled the moonwalk. The floor in the middle of the room creaked and groaned loudly as he slid backwards towards the far wall. To my 'untrained' ear it sounded like his feet were going to punch through any step. The massive spaceship's lights flashed continuously. Davinci didn't seem concerned in the least as he spun a pirouette 360 at the far end of the room just before his pile of art supplies and fluidly continued the quasi-moonwalk back towards me as he flipped and twirled the bag of *blue tahoe* like a baton.

He began chanting "To da moon! To da moon! To da moon!" As his moonwalk turned into more of a pow wow cat-like bounce. Davinci could *dance*.

His feet where still physically on the ground but I wouldn't have been a bit surprised if he would have lifted off the ground and hovered slowly up towards the ceiling.

"Ok Davinci, have fun on the moon bud, it was an honor meeting you."

I was in complete awe of the guy. The hype wasn't overblown.

"Wait, I pack ship."

He pulled a spaceship sculpture that looked very similar to the spaceship in the middle of the room, although much smaller, from a pile of canvas in the far corner. He then loaded the carved out bowl in the middle of the saucer with a nug from the bag and held the spaceship out toward me. He smiled.

"You better hit that first Davinci I wouldn't know where to begin."

He pulled a painted lighter out of his pocket, lit the bowl as he inhaled through the exhaust pipes on the back of the spaceship. The lights flashed. Dan took a rip that would have blown out the lung of a mortal man, closed his eyes as he held it in for upwards of a minute. When he finally exhaled he held the spaceship out towards me. I took a rip and was pleasantly surprised at how perfectly the ornate pipe hit.

"How much for the spaceship pipe?"

"Pipe not for sale. Only Davinci has license to drive space pipe!"

"Of course, of course, well I better be going to my next delivery, take care Davinci."

Dan was already back dancing, bouncing around in circles as he hit the space pipe continuously.

I couldn't help but smile as I walked towards the door, turning to take one last look at the old man bouncing around without a care in the world, the floor beneath him buckling like an October layer of Minnesota lake ice.

Back on ground level in front of Davinci's building, I studied the map, trying to get my bearings on the next delivery. It appeared to be on the Lower East Side. I found a subway stairwell and soon was on the 1 blazing south towards the bottom of the island. I hopped off at Sheridan Square, rode east, through Washington Square Park. Jaco. I noticed a tile signature above the far roof-line left by the notorious *space invader*. It was around 9:30 at night by this point, the streets were bustling with people. The late dinner crowd, the early late night crowd, the city was pulsing with life. I found the cross streets the address was on, I was close. I rounded another corner onto a quiet side street and stopped to read the map underneath a streetlight. Suddenly, a man jumped from behind a parked car and bum rushed me. He tackled me off the bike and I crashed hard to the pavement. I reached for the canister of bear spray I had attached to my right ankle, got a hold of it just as he was pouncing on me and blasted him in the face. And again. And again. And again. He quickly went down grabbing for his eyes, writhing around on the ground in agony. I got over the top of him and basted the poor bastard in a thick layer of spray. When he was completely incapacitated, I emptied his pockets. I took everything of value. Even his shoes. It was soon apparent up to this point in his career he had been a very successful mugger.

I gave away the loot I'd taken off of him to homeless folks on the street. One lucky junkie got a Rolex. As far as I was concerned it was all tainted for me, for them it was *free*. I got rid of everything except for the softball sized roll of cash. I had a better plan to disperse that.

I stood out front of 222 Bowery and compared the address with the one on my delivery list. They matched. It was a rundown place. An alley separated it from the apartment building beside it. I walked up the steps and rang the bell. All was silent, then I heard commotion in the back of the house. Things were getting knocked over. Glass shattering. The noise migrated to the back yard, I heard the fence door swing open with a clatter. A few seconds later a fat man in a white robe with gray stripes wearing big floppy slippers came running out of the alley full tilt, hung a right, hauled ass down the sidewalk yelling at himself, "UNHITCH THE PIANO JERRY YOU FAT FUUUCK!!"

I watched him running down the block. The front door swung open. A polar bear of a woman towered in the doorway. She hobbled out onto the front step and yelled down the block at Jerry through a makeshift newspaper bullhorn. "GET YOUR PANSY ASS BACK HEEEERE JERRY! IT'S JUST THE WEEEEED GUY!" She turned towards me. "Ol' Jer is running from a horde of bill collectors that grows by the day, if he so much as hears a bird shit on the sidewalk he's out the back running for the gad dang Hudson."

Jerry was walking towards us panting like a dog. A huge man, his enormous gut caused him to almost waddle. He had a black mustache perched on his round face, huge square plastic half inch thick glasses that magnified his eyes as if he was in a fishbowl, curly black hair around the outside of his head with nothing on top. On his feet he wore floppy slippers that looked like they'd been put through a garbage disposal. He was smiling a big smile. I counted three teeth missing. "Startled me...thought you were someone else. Here, I'll teach you the secret knock so you don't give me an aneurysm next time." Jerry tapped once....waited...then three quick knocks, waited....knocked twice...waited...knocked four times...then began wrapping on the door with both hands to the beat of a song I didn't recognized as he stared at me with googly eyes, bopping his head to the beat.

"Got it?" he said when he was finished.
"No."

Jerry went through the minute long secret knock again.

"There's no way I'm going to remember that Jer."

"Ok fuck it...come on in."

I walked into the entryway. It was stacked wall to wall, floor to ceiling with Amazon delivery boxes. "Come on in," Jerry said as he walked through the narrow pathway into the living room. His mangled slipper caught the edge of one stack of boxes, it wobbled back and forth, then toppled over. As Jerry tried to avoid getting buried, his legs got tangled in the falling boxes. He staggered desperately, trying to regain his balance, then tripped, lunging his massive body forward. He came down on top of the oak coffee table sitting in the middle of the room cracking it cleanly in half.

"Uuuufta!!" Jerry groaned.

"What's that Jer? You ok down there?"

The polar bear and I waded through the boxes, towards the smashed table.

"Good to go." Jerry bellowed as he rolled onto his back, groaning loudly.

"GOOD GOING JERRY! THAT WAS MY GRANDMOTHERS TABLE!" yelled the polar bear.

Jerry battled his way to his feet groaning, huffing, puffing all the way. He stood, silent. His magnified, googly eyes darting around the room. Mouth wide open, speechless.

I took the order out of my pack. A half zip *lemon meringue*, a half zip *blue tahoe*. "That'll be 250$." Jerry undid his robe, reached into his 'undergarments', pulled out a rubber-banded wad of bills. "Don't worry it's all there counted it *many* times." Jerry said with a nervous smile. I hesitantly grabbed the bundle that looked like it contained mostly one's.

"What are you a stripper Jerry?"

Jerry stood there looking confused, eye's darting around in circles.

"Are you sure you're alright that was quite the tumble you took?"

"Breakfast." Jerry said as he picked up the bag of *blue tahoe*, unzipped it, and took in a long slow whiff with his eye's closed. "Hmmmmmm... that's that gas." He said as he danced a little jig amid the shards of table.

It was 10:15 when I finished the deliveries. I flipped open the flipper. A message from Truman, "at Bar Centrale, stop by when you're finished." I hopped on the F train rumbling back towards Midtown, got off at 45th. I walked into an old Italian restaurant and asked the hostess if she could point me in the direction of Centrale. She gave me a double take when I said Centrale, but pointed it out on my map.

"How the hell do you think you're getting in there?"

"No idea." I said as I walked out the front door.

I was in front of a brownstone in Midtown West. A wide brick staircase led up to two redwood double doors. There was no sign above the door. I noticed a few guys lurking across the street with cameras. I called Truman. No answer. The doors swung open, there he was. We smoked a J on the front steps, then walked inside. Once we made it through the doors, past the doormen, there were several layers of thick velvet curtains. When we emerged from the curtains, Pen and Teller appeared to be sitting at the corner table to our left. *How high was I?* It was a cozy place. A dozen or so small booths with a bar in the corner. It was dimly lit, with the ambiance of a speak easy. We walked to a booth. There were four people sitting at the table. Truman went around the horn and introduced me. On one side sat Zach. I recognized him, I had seen him in a number of shows and films. He had written directed and starred in a film in his late 20's that had become a cult classic. Next to Zach sat Sofia. She was mid twenties, beautiful, Italian, and had just landed a role opposite a well known actor in an action flick. On the other side of the table were Nick and Amanda. Nick was the lead in *A Bronx Tale* on Broadway and Amanda owned a well known fitness company.

"How did the deliveries go?"

"Well, I was attacked by a dog, watched a drag-clown get thrown through a wall by a mechanical horse, and a large man attempted to mug me. Decent first night on the bike."

The table howled with laughter.

"One bright spot was meeting my new hero 'Davinci' the UFO artist."

"Who?"

"Dan Davinci... let's just say he sells his art *outside* the Outsider Art Fair..."

After dinner we swam through the sea of curtains into the calm summer twilight. It had cooled just enough to be pleasant. We lingered on the front steps as a few of the group enjoyed after dinner darts to complete their wine buzz. The lone paparazzi peered over at us trying to pin down if anyone was worth anything. Up the block to our left there seemed to be a commotion moving toward us down the sidewalk. A swarm of camera's flashed and popped around a woman. It was hard to tell who it was. Soon, Rihanna walked past the front steps of Centrale down two more storefronts, into a Brazilian grill. The horde of photographers buzzed around her until she was inside the front doors. We walked past them undisturbed, towards the bright lights of Broadway.

The next day Truman, George and I went for a late-morning walk along the Hudson. We smoked joints, walked, talked. Caught up. When we got down past midtown I told Truman we needed to head inland, I needed to get to the Empire State building. Not for sightseeing. It was another warm muggy day but the clouds had started to thicken up which helped make it comfortable. After another hour of walking we stood at the base of the iconic building. I told Truman and George to wait over on a bench, I would be back in fifteen minutes. George seemed happy about the break. After riding the elevator to the top, I walked over to the railing, pulled out the fat ball of cash from the mugger. I hadn't counted the money but I estimated there was somewhere around 5 grand. Lots of bills. I removed the thick rubberband, launched the cash off the railing, out into the city. The cash exploded like confetti and floated, fluttered lazily toward the busy silence below. I ran for the elevator to get back down to the street for the show.

It was mayhem down on street level. Raining Benjamins. Traffic had come to a halt. It looked like someone had let the animals out of the circus. Standing on car hoods, jumping, diving, fighting. Hordes of people were migrating towards the Empire from all directions. Cops blowing whistles trying to regain order. I walked over to Truman and George, I couldn't tell who was more excited. "Time for us to roll boys!" Truman had a handful of hundreds in one hand. He gave me a confused look, then a huge smile. "You?"

I turned to look at the circus, which was spiraling out of control. Truman left the wad of cash in an old hobos hands and the guy handed him a fat joint with a strange wink as we walked south for a few blocks and then ducked back down into the subway.

We made our way to Central Park and agreed to meet at the cast party atop the Empire Hotel around ten. I walked northeast through the park towards the Guggenheim. The featured exhibition was on Chinese art in the 20th Century. I spent most of my time staring at the only Van Gogh. I wandered back past the Met, into the Park, stopping off for a coffee and baguette at the Le Pain Quotidien cafe tucked into a hill in the eastern interior of the park. When I made it to the south edge of the park I decided to hop on the subway and head towards pier 1 for sunset. I hopped on the A and in 20 minutes walked up into the mango colored sky framing Lady Liberty.

I found a bench, sat, pulled out the joint compliments of the hobo. I lit it. A light breeze blew off the sparkling water. I put on jazz and watched the blazing sun sink like a ship into the Atlantic. When the last sliver had vanished, I realized I was already late for the party. I hurried over to the subway, hopped on the first train that showed up.

After staring at the map near the sliding doors for a few minutes trying to decipher where this damn thing was going, the lines on the map started dancing around on the page. The longer I looked, the more of a maze it was. A continuously moving maze with dancing lines. I sat back in a bench seat and fell into a trance amid the blur of movement as we rumbled along underneath the city. When I heard we were in the 100's I decided to get off for some reason. Where was I trying to get to again? I was beginning to suspect that the joint from the bum had been dipped in *PCP! Fine by me.*

Topside, the vivid colors and blur of movement made it feel like I was in a kaleidoscope. I found a busy street, stumbled out into traffic as I hailed a cab. "Empire Hotel!" Time had lost meaning. The earth was spinning faster than normal.

As we pulled up to the Empire I spotted Truman dancing in the lobby. He had *one-centillion* running shorts on, tall multi-colored socks, high tops, a hand-painted t-shirt with a light brown duffel bag slung across his chest. He was *fully tuned.* I had passed *Pluto* somewhere around midtown. I walked in, we headed for the elevator. Truman punched the button with a dancing R on it. We popped out onto the roof and once cleared by security, joined the party.

We walked up a small set of stairs to the pool. As we walked around to open chairs on the opposite side we passed Kristen Chenoweth. She gave Truman a hug. "Who's your friend?" We chatted for a bit then her boyfriend showed up and swooped her away. We found some open chairs next to the pool by two beautiful ladies. One of them asked 'how the hell we got in' and Truman managed to convey that he was in the show as he swayed back and forth like a character from mortal combat when the narrator is chanting 'finish him.' For some reason they were hesitant to believe him, maybe it was the duffel bag. They turned to me to confirm or deny. I was nearly starting to formulate an answer when Truman broke into a solo from Jersey boys (he had played Bob Gaudio a few years back) as he threw his head back and swayed in small circles. The entire party came to a halt and listened in awe. It sounded like Bob himself was on the roof. Truman was damn near blacked out serenading (in perfect pitch) the entire rooftop. Duffel bag and all. Applause erupted across the rooftop and the look on the girls faces was pure shock.

In my pocket I found the remainder of the laced joint. I walked to the edge of the rooftop, lit it, leaned back and gazed into the star filled sky. To the moon!

All I remember after that point is various colors and sounds. A vivid night in New York City.

I woke up on the couch in Truman's living room. George was sitting on the armrest wagging his tail. It was a warm soupy morning, a cool breeze blew in gently through the window from the shade of the alley. Truman was in the kitchen cooking breakfast. Egg omelets with Italian sausage, garlic, onions, peppers, mushrooms, with arugula on top. I brewed Kingston coffee, fired up the bong and before long we were recovered from the previous evening and ready for another summer day in the city. It was Truman's day off and it was my last full day in town. My flight to San Francisco departed from JFK the next morning at 7:00 am.

Truman's phone lit up. It was Zach, he invited us to drop by his place in Midtown. We rolled a few J's for the road, filled George's dish with the leftovers from breakfast.

He was happy as a clam. We walked to the Subway, hopped on the A and in 15 minutes we were outside a fancy Midtown high-rise. Truman rang the security box next to the door, soon we heard a buzz as the door unlocked. The lobby was marble, granite and gold. We walked to the elevator. Truman punched the top floor. The elevator opened into the apartment. As we walked in, the knight armor from *G. State* appeared to be standing at attention near the window facing the river. How high was I? We fired up the joints and told stories. Zach was directing a movie with three old well known actors and the tales he had from working with them were great.

At some point we left Zach's and the afternoon was basically a New York Haze. I can only remember bits and pieces, fragments in time and space. The bag from Manchini was rolled up into 15 large joints, and one by one, I smoked them while walking, and then eventually floating around the island of Manhattan. This is what I remember.

I was on a rooftop on the upper east side. An all you can eat Sushi restaurant. I was up in a tree in Central Park. I was out on the end of a dock on the Westside Riverfront, then on the deck of a Yacht. They dropped me at Lady Liberty, I smoked a J in her torch. I was out on Governors Island rolling in the grass. I was riding a bike through Times Square, cars honking, swerving. I jumped off the bike as it was about to be hit by a yellow cab. The bike went off the hood, flipped through the air and flew into the grill of a city bus, then was mangled like a paperclip underneath the bus and spit out the back crunched into a ball. I watched from the sidewalk as I smoked a joint. I walked into a shop and bought a pair of rollerblades, began rollerblading through stopped traffic in the clogged roads in the heart of the city. I rollerbladed into a restaurant and was asked to leave. I grabbed onto the back of a city bus and was pulled 50 blocks north where I found myself in the Cloisters, a very nice quiet park. Across the water I spotted some potential ski lines on the rocky hillside. I rollerbladed from one end of a subway train to the other.

Back at 72nd and Broadway, Truman cooked dinner while I chain-smoked joints. George looked like he was enjoying his second hand high over on the couch.

Seared salmon, roasted sweet potatoes, and a sauteed medley of asparagus with olives, basil and bacon. We threw on an old ski movie. A little known classic called *The Game.* It had inspired us to start skiing back when we were kids and the cast had started the freeride ski movement. The godfathers of modern skiing. Mike Douglas, JP Auclair, Vincent Dorian, Seth Morrison, Candide and of course Plake. Before these guys skiing was a bunch of old rich stiffs with one piece yellow snow suits wedged up their ass.

The mellow evening sun lit up the haze into a peach glow. Sitting there eating the delicious meal next to Truman and George, I soaked in the moment. It reminded me what it felt like to have a family. It was why I'd come here in the first place. Truman asked about the next leg of my journey. I told him I was heading for Yosemite National Park. *The John Muir trail.* Into the Mountains. I was walking into the wilderness. George stared back at me like I was crazy. I couldn't blame him.

I packed up my suitcase. George hopped up, cuddled in my lap. He knew what the packing meant. He stared at me with that under-bite and those big sad eyes and I couldn't help but love him. It was one in the morning and I figured I better start riding the rails towards JFK for my 7:00 am flight in a few hours so Truman and I stayed up smoking J's, drinking coffee, playing with George in the haze and enjoying the time we had left together.

A tear slid down my cheek as I rode the elevator down to the street. The laughs of the past few days had lifted my spirit, days bathed in luxury before the shit show that lay ahead. The road was out there waiting for me.

28

Whispering to me. Seducing me with its freedom and unpredictability. Sometimes you just want to see for yourself what lies behind the misty curtain. If I would have known what lay ahead, I never would have gotten on that plane.

Free Doug

San Francisco - Yosemite

I peered out the oval window, through dark misty clouds I could see glimpses of it 20,000 feet below. A smoky orange twilight haze hovered over the Pacific on the horizon, shadows consumed the shivering mountains below leaving them in an ominous state of semi-lit darkness. Snow was still clinging to the highest peaks even in mid-July. In a few days, or however long it took me to get to Yosemite from San Francisco, this shadow land of soaring peaks, ice cold lakes, redwoods, bobcats, bears, rattlesnakes, whitewater and *absolute freedom* would be my home for the next several months. The Sierra wilderness was down there waiting for me, waiting to eat me alive. It probably would, I didn't care. I was going to hike north until the *wheels fell off*.

We landed in San Francisco around 11:00 pm. I grabbed my pack from the overhead compartment, waited for the slow procession off the plane. As I walked through the terminal towards the security checkpoint, I realized I was about to walk into a whole different kind of wilderness. I decided to stay overnight and enter the city of fog in the light of day when I stood a chance. I found a spot near the gate for a flight heading to China at 2:00 am, curled up amongst the Chinese passengers, then tossed and turned in a dreamless restless sleepless haze until the sun came up.

The lack of sleep and fresh surroundings propelled my mind into a manic state and once again I was ready for anything. I grabbed a steaming coffee, headed for the BART. Before I left San Francisco for Yosemite I needed to round up trail supplies, cannabis, and stop by the public library to print off the trail maps for the John Muir Trail so I knew where in the *lively fuck* I was going. As we rumbled down the tracks through the foggy morning I asked the lady beside me what stop to get off for the library. "Three more stops...good luck, you're going to need it."

When I emerged from the subway into the daylight, the fog had burned off and it was blistering hot. Not a cloud in the California sky. It was a different shade of blue than I was used to. I walked into the land of the homeless. I was one of them. Everywhere I looked, sad, ragged, worn down souls with crazed desperate eyes roamed like zombies. I already missed New York City. The homeless there were happily sedated on strong opiates and didn't seem to have an ounce of fight left in them. These vagrants were like wild animals, vultures ready to swarm any whiff of fresh meat they could devour. I put my head down and tried to fit in. Somehow they could smell resources on me and in the 5 blocks to the library I was swarmed and begged for handouts 14 times. I threw one guy half a sandwich, it disappeared almost before it hit his hands. I walked into the San Francisco Public Library, approached the lady at the front desk. She was a heavy gal in her 50's that looked like she'd given up a long time ago. "Hi, I need to print off trail maps could you point me in the right direction?"

"Here's a guest pass 5th floor up the stairs take a right, good luck finding a computer, and good luck with that trail..." she said as she looked down, raising her eyebrows.

The library was swarming with bums looking for an oasis from the sweltering heat. After 45 minutes of hovering, I was finally able to snag an open computer. I pulled up the John Muir Trail topographic trail maps. They were made by some guy that called himself *halfmile* and had made it his life's work to give hikers the best chance of survival as they wandered off into the wilderness. He included every imaginable detail you should or could know while hiking. Where the water was, where the best spots to camp were, where the wild animals were most likely to attack, where the best views were. Everything. He was truly an artist and probably crazy. Without his maps you didn't stand a chance. I punched in the section of trail that I planned to hike which started in Tuolumne Meadows and went a thousand miles north somewhere into northern Oregon. I had no idea how far I would make it, but figured I better have the maps in case I survived that long. The print screen appeared for the section I had selected, it was 95 pages. I clicked print. The printer was in a small office room in the back corner of the 5th floor. It was big, old, and looked like it had been used and abused for far longer than it deserved. It fired up, started on the largest continuous job it had attempted in years...
"Reeee....Ruuuuuu...Reeeee......Ruuuuuu....Reeee....Ruuu"
It sounded like a dying animal being tortured as it groaned and screeched through the first 25-30 pages without a hitch. Then it started to heat up... A warning message began flashing on the old scratched up display screen -FAN MALFUNCTION SYSTEM OVERHEATING SHUT DOWN IMMEDIATELY- (I thought these things shut down automatically when they overheated...but this thing

was *ancient!*). I pushed the cancel button, nothing happened. I held it again for longer this time. Nothing. I tried the power button. It kept spitting out pages... I looked for the power source but it was plugged in way back behind large oak cabinets, impossible to reach. "Reeeeee...Ruuuuuuuuuuuuuuu...Reeee....Ruuuuuuuuuu." It kept plugging away but it was struggling, starting to bog down now. The amount of heat it was putting out was *amazing*. It smelled like a car battery roasting on a bonfire. I looked around for help, there weren't any library workers in sight, but a few bums working on the computers near mine had noticed the smell. "Damn son...that thing smells like shiiiiit, shut 'er down 'fore she goes up'n flaaames!"

"I'm trying the damn thing won't shut down!"

Thick smoke started coming from somewhere deep inside the screeching machine. "I'll go for help, you guys try to get at that cord!"

"We gone!"

They collectively started hobbling towards the stairwell.

The printer was making a growling sound now and the smell was unbearable. Finally it went silent. The screen was black, as were the edges of the last several pages it had spit out. I looked around, the 5th floor was deserted, the hobos had run for the exits. A smoky haze hung in the air. I thought about what to do for a moment and then it was clear. I grabbed the smoldering stack of pages, stuffed them into my pack, headed for the stairs. As I ran down the first flight two stairs at a time, a small army of short, fat, maintenance workers were huffing and puffing up, armed with fire extinguishers.

"Did you see where the smoke is coming from!?"

"The printer in the back room on the 5th floor! Some bum tried to print a 95 page job!"

Back out on the street you could have cooked a steak on the sidewalk. No wonder these vagrants were so wild and desperate, they were being *cooked alive*! I was three blocks north of the library when two firetrucks came roaring and blaring around the corner headed straight for the library.

I needed to round up a tent, backpackers pack, stove, whatever else I would need to survive out on the trail. Oh, and a sleeping bag, I had tried to wash mine in a commercial washer at the laundromat and it had ground it into a wet pile of *confetti*. I wandered deliriously through the heat for an hour searching for a camping store. Finally, I stumbled upon a North Face store on Post St. I found the items on my list including a bag that was rated to keep you alive down to 0 degrees. As I was checking out the cashier asked if I had a trip planned.

"I'm heading for the JMT".

"My friend has been out on the PCT since May," he said. "She started on the Mexican border. Hopped off the trail to drop by for a visit on her way past here a few weeks ago, said it's no joke out there. They got trapped in a snowstorm for a week on a mountain pass near Whitney, almost ran out of food. One of them was bitten by a rattlesnake out in the Mohave, another fell into a rushing river, floated a mile downstream before he snagged on an overhanging tree branch and was able to drag his frozen ass back on dry land."

"Sounds like things are going smoothly, did she head back out?"

"Far as I know she's back out there, slogging north."

Damn, I thought as I walked out the front doors onto Post street. Do I have everything I need for the battle that lay ahead? Nope, there was one thing I had forgotten. I ran back in and bought a shit shovel, with all that trouble lurking out there...wouldn't want to leave a turd behind.

It was late afternoon. I found a coffee shop to rest while I figured out where I was going to sleep. I decided to try Love. I sent her a text. I asked the barista if there were any hostels in the neighborhood. She pointed me in the direction of the SF Central Hostel, said she had stayed there when she first got into town.

I found the SF Central Hostel without a problem. It was an old black and white building. The lobby was vintage 1920's, bustling with young people. Hippies, Hipsters, YP's, dirtbags, foreigners, this place had them all. It was full of life. Maybe I could learn something here. I checked in at the front desk, snagging the last bed available in the whole place. Luck seemed to be on my side. I was going to need it. My room was on the top floor. It was simple, two bunks in the main room, a bathroom connected, and a window with a view of the street below. I peered out the window. Across the street a man in a tattered camo jacket with long hair and no legs rolled his wheelchair out the lobby doors of his apartment building and down the sidewalk. He reached into his pocket, pulled out a cigarette, lit it. A few people stopped to chat as they passed by on their way into the building. I looked down the quiet street. I couldn't quite see the ocean.

Long shadows danced on the sidewalk as the Palm trees bent in the hot winds. I decided to go for a walk. As I made my way west, San Francisco began to look charmed. The heat of the day had baked the energy out of the street folk and everyone I passed seemed relaxed and calm. Maybe they had just found their drugs. I walked down Golden Gate Ave past Jefferson Square Park. A bum was fast asleep on a park bench. On the opposite side of the park a mom and daughter flew a kite. The kite fluttered and floated in the breeze like it didn't have a care in the world. Not far from me a guy tossed a frisbee for his black lab. I took off my shoes, walked barefoot through the grass. There wasn't any dew on it but it was nice and cool. I continued west on Golden Gate ave, then hopped down a couple blocks and there they were. *The painted ladies.* I wanted to get a glimpse of the sun dipping below the horizon on the bay but I couldn't seem to get high enough to get a good vantage. I had read about San Frans 11 mystic hills but couldn't find them. It was getting dark, I walked back towards the hostel, stopping off for noodles on the way.

My roommates were back when I showed up. A young couple in their early 20's, Kiera and Thomas. Aussies. They had flown into LA and were currently on the first leg of their journey around the states headed up the west coast, then east towards Chicago and New York. I lay in the quiet stillness, but couldn't fall asleep right away. Then I heard some rustling in the bunk across the room, then quiet rhythmic moaning. The Aussies were fucking. She was really getting it good, finally they both let out a moan.

I woke up around 9 the next morning. The Aussies were gone. I peered out the window, the fog had burned off and it was another hot cloudless day. I showered, packed my backpack and made my way down to the kitchen. The kitchen was bustling with activity. I managed to toast a couple of bagels, pour a cup of coffee and find a spot in the corner. I sat studying the map of San Francisco I had found on the rack of brochures in the lobby. The only item I had left on my to do list before I could head for the hills was to find a fat sack of cannabis for the trail. This was long before weed was legal in California, but it was California, how hard could it be? As I studied the maps I noticed Golden Gate Park was straight west of me, and located smack dab in the middle of the park there it was, *Hippy Hill*.

The long slog through the morning heat took everything I had. My pack felt like it weighed 100 pounds, the 17 blocks west to the park took almost 2 hours. How in the *lively fuck* was I going to carry this damn thing 1000 miles north over 12,000 ft. mountains? I'd cross that bridge when I got there, first I needed to get *high*.

I was in the Haight Ashbury District, almost to the park. As I entered the far east edge of the park, I took a glance at my map. It looked to me like the famous hill I was looking for was directly in front of me, I collapsed on a park bench. The park was quiet, two joggers passed by. An old couple walked their golden lab lazily down the path. A few teenagers skateboarded on a set of steps, trying to slide the rails. Two days earlier I had been sitting on a bench on the opposite coast on the west edge of Central Park. They couldn't have been more different. Central Park was lush, magical, inspiring. This place felt burnt out, scorched, like the magic had once been here but since moved on. A disheveled, desperate looking lady approached me. "Got any weed I could buy?" she asked.

"Nope, is this a good place to find some?"

"This is probably the best place in all of San Francisco to buy weed...it's still early, wait until this afternoon." she said as she wandered off aimlessly.

I sat on the bench in front of *Hippy Hill* waiting for the pot dealers of San Francisco to get to their storefront. They were late. Maybe I was early. I decided to take a stroll and see more of the park. A dirt path led me through a patch of pine trees towards JFK drive, across the street was the Conservatory of Flowers. As I approached the road I noticed a brightly colored hand-painted old V.W. van with two surfboards fastened to the top parked in a no parking zone. One tire was completely over the curb in the grass and a young couple was laying motionless in the lawn staring up at the summer sky. Jackpot. I walked over to the van. "You folks wouldn't happen to have any extra green that you could sell would you?" The guy slowly sat up, he was early 20's, had long brown hair, no shirt, homemade shorts and thong sandles on.

"Yooooo duuuuuddddee whaaaaaat up, I'm Cheswick. O yaaaa we've got some greeeeen for you maaaan. This hydroponic hits like a freeeeight traaaaaain." He unzipped the duffle bag that was laying in the grass between them. It had at least a pound of dense nugs all bagged up ready to go.

"I'll take a **qp**."

"Right on!"

Cheswick grabbed a few pre-weighed bags, handed them to me as I handed him a wad of cash. He counted the cash, then handed me back a few 20's.

Kylie, baaabe, roll us up a faaaattie let's get Jack baaaaked out of his goooord." Kylie sat up. She was stunningly beautiful. She had long blond hair, piercing sky blue eyes and a cute button nose. Her skin had a rich midsummer tan, she wore a thin flowery sundress and clearly wasn't wearing a bra. She looked at me with a stony smile and reached into the duffle bag, pulled out a grinder, rolling papers, and rolled up an enormous joint. We puffed and passed, puffed and passed, puffed puffed puffed and passed. All we could do was lay in the shade from the van in a state of bliss. A butterfly floated and fluttered in short jerky spurts above my head. The leaves on the trees danced playfully in the hot breeze. Way off in the distance I could faintly hear the quiet roar of the ocean. After who knows how long I was able to stand up and pick up my pack. I thanked my new friends and wished them peace, love, happiness, all that good hippie shit. Now I was ready for the *High Sierra*...in this realm *anything* was possible. My pack felt lighter, all the pain was gone. I traversed my way back across the park climbing and descending *Hippy Hill* (elevation 25 ft.).

It was mid-afternoon now and the park had come to life. Groups of long haired hippies lounged in the grass all over the hill and across the entire park keeping the tradition alive. Large puffs of white smoke rose into the air above the groups. A tall curvy woman danced with long colorful ribbons whirling in circles then switching directions spinning back where she came from. Everyone seemed happy and peaceful. A beautiful scene. It felt like I had gone back in time. *Hippy Hill* had delivered, maybe the magic hadn't left after all.

I walked into the neighborhood south of the park. What was I looking for? I had no idea. I was content wandering aimlessly. Old Victorian homes lined the narrow streets. Jazz floated through the air intermittently. I stopped in a convenience store and bought ten lighters. Survival tools. Something was rumbling down the street behind me. I turned around, a trolley was barreling down on me. I leapt out of the way just in time and before I knew what I was doing I had boarded and was blazing down the tracks. *How high was I?* I turned to the lady next to me. She was old, sophisticated, academic looking, a college professor.

"Where is this thing going?"

She took one look at me, smiled and said, "Well, depends how long you stay on board but it will take you to Fisherman's Wharf if you stay on until end of the line. Where are you trying to go?"

"Not sure if I'm foot or horseback at this point."

She laughed. "Hippy Hill will do that to you. I'd say head towards the Wharf, it looks out over the bay across the water to Oakland, it will be beautiful at sunset."

We entered a tunnel, the light was snuffed out. When we popped back into the light we were in the heart of the city. Skyscrapers lined the street on both sides and crowds of people swarmed the storefronts and street vendors. We slowed to a stop, she got up to leave.

"Enjoy the fog."

The trolley continued to rumble along, up and down steep hills, blazing down the tracks. The buildings and people one colorful blur. Pink infused sunlight flashed in and out as it poured through the gaps in the buildings. I looked at the map sitting in my lap. I didn't need a map. This trolley was taking me exactly where I needed to go. We made another stop. There was a park surrounded by tall buildings with mirrored windows from top to bottom. I caught the reflection of the ocean rolling on the side of one of the buildings. I grabbed my pack and hopped off the trolley.

Across the park past the buildings and storefronts, the waterfront opened up before me, there it was. The Pacific Ocean glistening and sparkling in the golden-red dusk, the Oakland hills looming across the bay. The view was mystical. Two days earlier I had been sitting at pier 1 on the southwest tip of Manhattan watching the same sun set beneath Lady Liberty.

I found a bench to sit on the edge of the waterfront walkway, set down my pack, unzipped the top pocket and found my bowl, lighter and cannabis. I packed a bowl to the brim. Four rips later I was back on the moon. The cool salty breeze was refreshing. I sat there listening to hazy Jazz, watching the sun fade into the Pacific. Then I remembered Love. I had texted her the previous day but hadn't checked my phone since to see if she'd gotten back to me. Sure enough there was a new text from Love.

"Of course you can stay here! Welcome to the Bay area! Call me and we'll arrange a place for me to come pick you up. We live across the Bay in the Oakland hills."

I gave her a call. She said to hop on the BART, take it to Fruitvale Station across the water. Soon I was blazing across the bay.

I got off the BART at Fruitvalle station, walked towards the entrance. I noticed a girl that seemed to be waiting for a ride as well. She seemed familiar. Suddenly I remembered, she was Loves daughter Anne, I had met her in Brooklyn with Love. I walked over to her, she looked up from her phone and smiled. "Hey Jack! Small world! Welcome to Oakland!"

A few minutes later, a black *M. Benz* pulled into the pickup area. "Here she is." The trunk opened. I loaded my pack into the back and hopped in. Soon we were out of the city lights, winding our way into the hills surrounding the bay. We wound around curves up a hilly road with towering green oak trees lining either side. Long driveways guarded by ornate gates disappeared into the hills. We slowed, took a right as a latticed brass gate opened into a long cobblestone driveway. The driveway was lined by tall Monterey pines on either side. We continued to wind our way up into the hills. After a mile, the narrow driveway opened up, perched on a hill above the driveway sat an immaculate Victorian era mansion. It had two looming towers, one was round the other square, a large balcony wrapped around the second story. Columns with ornate spindle work framed the front and a large porch led up to the door. It was white with blue and cherry red lined windows and trim. We hopped out of the G-wagon, the city sparkling below us. As we made our way up to the porch the front door swung open, a man walked towards us. He wore khaki pants, a blue dress shirt with a wool sweater vest over the top.

"This is my husband Carl, this is Jack."

He extended his hand and smiled. "My wife seems to be pretty fond of you...I've got to say I was a little shall we say, skeptical when she said she was bringing home a 'traveler' she had met on the subway in Brooklyn but I feel a little better already, you don't look like much of a killer. Come on in dinner's on the table." We walked into the house and the aromas of steak, butter, fresh rolls, corn on the cob and cookies.

After dinner Love showed me to my room up in one of the towers. It was a very nice room, its own bathroom with a shower attached and a small door that opened to a balcony overlooking the bay. I hopped through the shower, put on some fresh clothes, then made my way downstairs where Love, John and Anne were sitting at the kitchen table. "Hey Carl or Love you wouldn't know of a train or bus that would take me to Yosemite from here or nearby would you?"

"I think the Amtrak will get you close, then a bus will take you into the park from Merced" said Carl. "A friend of mine was talking about it the other day, he had taken it into the park a few weekends ago to avoid traffic. Apparently the buses have their own lane and pass hours

worth of cars backed up waiting to get through the gate."
He opened his laptop, started punching keys. "Looks like
it's all one ticket you book through the Amtrak company.
They have two a day, one at 7:30 am and the other at 1:30
in the afternoon."

"You're welcome to stay here as long as you want
of course!" said Love.

We sat up telling stories, laughing, drinking tea,
eating cookies.

I walked out onto my balcony overlooking the
sparkling lights of Oakland, San Francisco across the bay.
The black water shimmered like a disco ball. The silver
moon glowing high in the sky. I packed a bowl, walked
back out sliding the glass door behind me and settled into a
chair on the balcony. A gentle breeze kept the embers
glowing.

I woke early, re-packed my backpack, walked
downstairs. Carl and Love were sitting at the table reading
the paper, drinking coffee. "Morning!" bellowed Carl in a
deep morning baritone.

"Good morning! I think I better head out on the
morning train, get into the park with enough time to get
camp set up in the light."

"Grab some coffee and breakfast, we better hit the
road." I filled up my thermos with coffee. Love handed me
two bagels and an orange wrapped in a paper towel.

"I'm going to worry about you out on that trail!"

"Thank you for everything Love!" I said as I gave
her a hug.

Carl and I loaded up in the *M. Benz*, circled down
the driveway to the main gate, which opened for us. Soon
we were back in the city. Carl turned left into the Amtrak
station. I grabbed my pack out of the back, then stuck my
hand out to shake Carl's hand. "I don't want no damn
handshake, give me a hug bud! You're welcome to stay
anytime. Be safe out on that trail." I gave Carl a hug, then
walked into the Amtrak station, bought a ticket from the

tall lady with big glasses at the window. Soon I was rolling down the tracks.

The train blazed southeast through the blue morning across California farm country, the Sierra Nevada Mountains looming on the eastern horizon. Strawberry, tomato, almond and lettuce fields glistened as the hot sun melted off the morning dew. Workers with large bucket hats hurried to get their work done before the heat of the day baked them alive. A few hours later the train stopped in Merced. There was an announcement that this is where all of the Yosemite bound passengers were to transfer to the Yarts bus waiting in the parking lot.

I found an aisle seat next to a nice looking lady in maybe her forties. She had dark hair, tan skin, she was short, stocky, with powerful looking legs primed for hiking. I could gather by her attire and the look of her well organized well used pack that she was extremely dialed and prepared for whatever hike she had planned.

Her name was Janis, she was from South Carolina, here for a five day trip to do a classic 40 mile loop in Yosemite. She had been backpacking for 20 years all over the world but Yosemite was her favorite place to spend time out on the trail. She asked me what my plans were. I told her I was starting at Tuolomne Meadows, hiking north on the John Muir Trail until the wheels fell off. She looked at me searching for an indication that I was kidding, then realized I wasn't.

"Well how many backpacking trips have you been on to get ready for this?"

"None, first time."

She looked at me with a very concerned look on her face.

"You know that's crazy right?"

"That's what I hear."

Over the next hour Janis frantically gave me a crash course on what she had learned in her 20 years of experience backpacking.

I looked out the window, the landscape had changed dramatically. Steep rock walls rose hundreds of feet on both sides and a river foaming with whitewater flowed alongside. We had merged into the bus lane and were passing dozens of cars waiting to get through the southwest gate of Yosemite National Park. Soon we approached the gate but instead of slowing down the bus driver found another gear and we roared past the ranger station without so much as a wave to the Rangers carefully checking each car. We continued to wind through the deep canyon, before long we were there. The iconic Yosemite Valley. Wonderland. Highland meadows carpeted with wildflowers. Deep, cold mountain lakes feeding rivers that flowed down the canyon. The lowlands gently rose to the foothills which were covered in a thick forest of oak, ponderosa pine, cedar, and white fir trees up to the base of the rugged sheer rock walls and granite domes that soared thousands of feet into the pure blue summer sky. Waterfalls shot off the top of the high cliffs, tumbling down the rock faces into the valley. It was a charmed magical landscape unlike anywhere I'd been.

The bus pulled into a driveway, slowed to a stop. We filed off the bus. Once my feet were standing on the valley floor I stood in awe as I turned 360 degrees to take it in. The landscape emitted so much power and beauty, it was overwhelming.

Peak summer season was in full swing and the place was crawling with people. Tuolumne meadows was north of the valley an hour and notoriously much less busy. I decided to head up to Tuolumne on the next shuttle, get camp set up before dark. It was late afternoon, the day had gone by like a puff of wind. I made my way over to the nearest shuttle stop across the parking lot. Deb was standing at the schedule board.

"We may have a little problem here, according to this, the last shuttle to Tuolumne for the day left 40 minutes ago."

"Let's hitchhike."

"Ok..." Deb said hesitantly, "I haven't hitchhiked for a long time but I guess we don't have much of a choice."

We walked down the road, set our packs in the gravel, stood side by side. I put my thumb out. An old red Subaru pulled over. We hopped in. Rob and Jenni were park employees with a few days off, heading up to Tuolumne for a three day backpacking trip. We curled up the narrow mountain roads steadily gaining elevation the whole way. The panoramas were more and more spectacular around every corner. Soon, we were pulling into a parking spot next to the Tuolumne Meadows general store. A small white cabin with a cafe connected. The cafe was closed for the day so we walked into the general store, bought pizza's, then found a spot at the picnic tables overlooking the meadow. This was a main re-supply spot for the Pacific Crest Trail through-hikers which was one and the same with the John Muir Trail for 250 miles in Yosemite. As we sat there, hikers began walking out of the woods a few hundred feet from where we were sitting. The kind of people that come right out of nowhere, and go right back into it. They looked like they had been to war. Their faces were dark with tan and dirt, the whites of their eyes a stark contrast. Their arms and legs were covered in cuts, scratches, mud, and blood. Most walked with limps favoring one leg or the other, wincing with each step. The relief on their faces as they dropped their dirty packs to the ground, the strain and weight finally gone. As I sat there looking at my clean pack, my gear that was fresh off the store shelf, I felt embarrassed and couldn't wait to be beaten to a pulp by the trail. Caked from head to toe in blood sweat and dirt. To become a trail warrior, *part of the club.*

I watched as a man in maybe his mid sixties emerged from the woods, limping gingerly towards our table winoing terribly with each step. "Damn back's acting up again...herniated disks or some buuuullshit..." he muttered as he collapsed on the bench beside me. He had lots of white hair, a big white beard, his skin was deeply tanned. His legs were gristled with muscle. They almost looked like racehorse legs the tendons and muscles were so defined. He had a warm smile and a twinkle in his eye. "Names Ron." he said as he extended his hand to shake mine.

"I'm Jack, this is Deb," I said.

I handed him a slice of pizza. Three bites later it was gone.

"Yeeaap, thee old trail is beating the ancient fuck out of ol' Ronny this year," he said with a long sigh.

"How are you carrying a 60 pound pack with a herniated disc?"

"That's a damn gooood question, doc told me to pack er in 200 miles ago but.... ahhhh *fuck it*. This is what I do every summer been doing it for 25 years...ever since I lost my wife and daughter." he said quietly. "I don't know what I'd do without this ol' trail..." He said as he looked at me with sad, tired eyes. We sat talking and eating for an hour. His tales from the trail were pure entertainment. The night in mid July 99' when he woke up to a bear's head coming through the front door of his tent, "It's a damn good thing I sleep with the bear spray duck taped to my hand or I'd be toast." Or the time when a vicious storm pinned him down for 5 days, 80 miles from anything and he managed to hike the last 50 on a sleeve of saltines and half a jar of peanut butter. Or the time he slipped down some falls and broke his ankle. He had fashioned crutches out of tree branches and crutched the last 40 miles to the next re-supply in 3 days. "What a *boondoggle* that was." he said as he raised his eyebrows.

I'll never forget what Ron told me before he picked up his pack, slung it onto his back and disappeared into the forest. "*I guarantee you won't be the same person when you walk off this trail as the one you were when you walked onto it.*" And then as suddenly as he had come into our lives, he was gone. Disappearing into the woods, on down the trail. "WIIND THE LIVELY FUCK UP YA OLD HORSE THIS HERE'S BEAR COUNTRY!" I heard from the edge of the trees as he disappeared.

After dinner Janis and I walked up into the campground to set up camp. The campers were a mixture of beaten, battered through-hikers who had decided to take a few days at this oasis to recover before the next leg. Also, several families with campers enjoying their summer vacation to Yosemite. We found a few open spots in the far corner tucked back in the woods away from everything. It was perfect. I went to work setting up my tent for the first time. It wasn't exactly smooth, but I got it up. Janis didn't even have a tent, in no time she had her tarp stretched between two trees. Sleeping pad and bag situated underneath. I crawled into my tent, rolled a joint. I lit it. Had to get that new tent smell out. I crawled out and walked back through the campground towards the meadow. Most sites had campfires blazing, groups gathered around lighting up marshmallows, drinking cold beer. Crackling logs and laughter filled the cool calm air. I passed the dugout amphitheater where a group of Europeans played some sort of drinking game on long benches, down a narrow path through thick trees which spit me out at the general store. It was dark, quiet, closed up for the night. I walked across the road, into the meadow. The outline of the jagged peaks of the Cathedral range against the burnt orange clear twilight sky. A chill went through my entire body. *The power this place emitted.* To the north was Lembert Dome. For the past two weeks I had watched the sun set behind the skylines of New York City and San Francisco. I was out in the wilderness. The wild. I wandered through the wildflowers into the middle of the meadow, slowly spun 360 degrees imagining John Muir out here all those years ago.

The next morning I woke to the dripping of raindrops on my tent. I unzipped the fly, peered out.

Everything was soaked. Puddles gathered water from all directions and miniature streams braided together to connect and rush towards lower ground. I had unknowingly set up camp on a fairly high patch of ground. I crawled back into the tent and for the most part everything was still dry. I could see puddles pressing up against the corners but somehow the tent material was keeping it out.

It rained solid for the next four days and nights. I spent them in one solid haze. Puffing, sleeping, studying trail maps, short walks down to the general store for food and coffee, then back up into the haze. *All the way up.* My campsite slowly started to flood. I reset my tent on the one patch of dry land that was left. On one of my evening walks down to the general store I passed the Euro's campsite, they were making the most of the weather. *Steaming drunk*, mud-wrestling in the slop. Empty booze bottles lined the picnic table. One of the tents was rocking back and forth frantically, two of the poles snapped in half.

On my fifth morning in Yosemite I awoke to a blue sky and that fresh wet stone smell that the forest has after a soaking of cold rain. After nearly 72 hours in a *hydroponic haze* at 7500 ft I was completely rested and fully adjusted to the altitude. After studying my maps thoroughly for the last five days I had come up with a plan. Load the fuck out of my pack with as much food as I could possibly fit, set a heading North until I hit highway 108 where I would hitchhike to the next re-supply opportunity. Between me and there lay 85 miles/17,000 ft of elevation change. I had no experience to go on but I guess that's the beauty of the trail. In essence it breaks life down to its simplest. You walk. If it's too hot, you walk. If it rains, you walk. If a storm blows through, you take cover anywhere you can, then you walk. If you get hurt, you walk. If you can't walk anymore, you crawl. You summon whatever is inside you to keep moving forward down the trail. If you stop moving, well, you won't last long. That resolution deep inside that would only come out if pushed to the absolute breaking point was all I was banking on in lieu of experience, training, knowledge, and sanity.

I decided to head out later that afternoon and try to hike the 5 miles to Glen Aulin High Sierra Camp before dark. I packed my sloppy tent, drying it off as best I could. After an hour, I had everything situated back in and on my pack. I heaved the massive pack up on my back and walked through the Tuolumne meadows campground for the last time. I passed the Euro's campsite, gave the two sitting on the booze bottle filled picnic table the peace sign on the way by to which they gave me drunken smiles and waved profusely. Their campsite looked like it had been hit by a hurricane. The tents were collapsed and lay under a thick layer of sludge. There wasn't a tent pole that hadn't been snapped. Bodies lay motionless in the piles of tents and mud. Muddy clothes were strewn everywhere, a deflated soccer ball smoldered in the fire ring. I found the path through the pines to the general store.

I bought every cliff bar they had, 53. Oatmeal, coffee, vanilla wafers, bread, a pizza, and a huge container of peanut butter. I figured the peanut butter could hold me over for awhile if I ran out of everything else. Calories. It wouldn't all fit into my backpack, so I stuffed the rest into the mesh North Face bag my sleeping bag had come in. As I was paying for my food I noticed a sign in the general store saying they required every backpacker in the park to buy or rent a 'bear safe' container which were essentially enormous cumbersome cookie jars. But they wanted a 100$ deposit for one which made my decision easy. I would fight the bears for my food.

After I had managed to secure the enormous mesh food bag on the outside of my pack, I cooked my pizza on the grill outside the general store. My last meal. Better load up on as many calories as my body could possibly hold before I wandered into the wilderness. The picnic area was quiet, the rain had scared off a large bunch of the campers and most of the through-hikers had already headed out for the day. After I stuffed the last of the pizza into my mouth, I heaved my pack onto my back. I thought it had been heavy before, with the food I was barely able to stand under its weight, let alone *walk*. Maybe I *should* cut that toothbrush in half. My body would adjust, I told myself, *either that or break down*. I made my way across the road, into the meadow. According to my soggy map, the trail-head was on the far side.

It was a partly cloudy fairly cool day, with a few dark clouds lingering. I was ¾ across the meadow when suddenly it started pouring to the west. I hunkered down under a patch of trees and pulled out my rain jacket, watching the rain advance across the meadow, the grass jerking under it, the stones going black, then the mud. I rolled and smoked a joint under my raincoat while I waited. The sun broke through the final shelf of clouds and bathed for a moment the dripping trees with blood, awash of color, as if the very air had gone to wine. I didn't have any way to tell the time, no watch, and the *flipper* didn't have even a hint of service. My best guess was around 3 o clock. I had between 6 and 7 hours before dark. Should I postpone until tomorrow? No, as soon as the rain stopped I was launching, *fuck it*. I was as ready as I was ever going to be. The rain stopped. The sun came out. I took one last look at the general store, walked the rest of the way through the meadow, over the bridge across the roaring Tuolumne river and up a small incline to the trail-head sign. *5.4 miles to Glen Aulin High Sierra Camp*. And then I launched into the great beyond, the deep, wild wilderness. The further I got from civilization the more at peace I was. There was nothing to decide anymore. Nothing more I could do about it. I had what was on my back to make it through this stunningly beautiful, dangerous country to the next re-supply. All that was ahead of me was the trail. I pushed play on my ipod and on the random setting the first song to play was "*young men dead.*"

The first few miles were easy, nice and flat alongside the river. I found my rhythm. After I was rolling, the endorphins where flowing and the feelings of bliss began to take over. My love affair with the trail had begun. After an hour or two, I saw an opening onto the beach of pebbles alongside the river. I took my pack off, decided it was time for a joint. When I was completely *torched*, I noticed across the river to the north was Lembert Dome. I wanted a photo at the beginning of my journey, a photo before and after whatever the trail did to me. Unless it finished me off of course, then there would just be the before...better make it a good one. I fished my camera out from the top pocket of my pack, positioned it on a log. I tried a few on the self photo timer setting but they weren't framed the way I wanted them. I snapped one without me in it. My pack resting on the pebble covered shores of the roaring Tuolumne, Lembert Dome looming in the background. I hiked on.

I made my way across the beach back out onto the trail, continued my walk. I walked without a break and fell into the trail trance, a meditative state where time and pain don't exist. When I came to, twilight was gathering against the Cathedral range. The tree's opened up as I walked out onto a granite slab. A stream cut through the granite for the next mile falling 1000 feet into a deep canyon where according to my map, the camp was. The canyon was surrounded on all sides by tall clay colored granite walls. I followed rock steps down alongside Tuolumne Falls and crossed the footbridge overlooking White Cascade, another set of falls, arriving at camp as dusk settled in.

The camp was bustling with activity. Campers cooking dinner, setting up tents. I didn't see any spots open, so I kept walking. The camp was full of backpackers. Some looked like they had been on the trail for months, some looked like they were just here for a few days. I walked along the river past the campground, found a spot overlooking a deep gorge with rapids flowing through it. I was able to get my tent set up just as the last of the light faded to night. I smoked a bowl, fell asleep to the soothing noise of the roaring stream ripping through the canyon below.

I woke in the cool morning blue, unzipped my tent door, crawled out of my tent and fired up my jet-boil to make oatmeal and coffee. It took longer than it should have, but I managed alright and enjoyed my breakfast overlooking the whitewater. After I packed up camp, I walked back down through the campground. It was still early, maybe 7:00, but most of the backpackers were up, cooking, eating, packing up camp. I stopped at the water spicket in the center of camp, filled up my water bottle and 5 liter pouch. My trail-maps had notes on where the best spots to get water were, or if there was a section of trail without reliable water sources. Water appeared to be plentiful on this section, at some point each day you were down in a canyon which had streams full of fresh snow melt-off running through them. I hiked on.

Before long, I drifted into the trail trance, following the trail north on the floor of a canyon, high pine forest blanketed the mountains on either side. Every couple hours I stopped to eat a cliff bar and smoke a joint. Sometime around mid-day I started passing south bound hikers who had been out on this section during the 4 days of rain. They looked like they been *through it*. Caked with mud from head to toe, the look on their faces told a story of brutality. I stopped to chat with a middle aged couple who looked like seasoned veterans of the trail. Tom and Sandy told me how they had hunkered down for a day and a half to wait out the rain but had no choice except to keep slogging down the trail to keep from running out of food. They had hiked for 2 ½ days through a monsoon. Both had slipped and tumbled down a steep section of trail, their arms and legs looked like they had gone down on a motorcycle. Trail rash. "Luckily we were able to self arrest on some bushes before it got really steep, could've been bad." said

Tom. I told them they were getting close to Glen Aulin. Looks of pure relief on their faces, they continued to limp south towards safety. I hiked on. North, into the wild. On my way out of camp that morning I had overheard a conversation about a possible storm heading our way, the group had been debating whether to stay close to the relative safety of Tuolumne meadows until it passed or continue on into the wilderness. I hiked on.

Late afternoon, the narrow tree-lined trail opened up into a highland meadow carpeted with flowers. As I walked into the clearing I noticed a guy laying in the tall grass, head resting on his pack, smoking a cigarette, reading a book. I stopped to say hi on my way past, he said something back to me in French, with a smile, thumbs up. I smiled, waved. I hiked on.

By early evening I had knocked off close to 8 miles. They had been as easy as miles come, flat canyons and meadows. I had been walking parallel to a stream all day. I came to my first crossing. It was too deep, moving too fast to wade through. I smoked a joint, studying the tangled mess of logs and trees that lay across it, trying to find the best route. These crossings, according to the limited research I had done on the trail, were among the most dangerous obstacles you would face out here, fall off a tree bridge and you could easily get caught in the current and rip downriver for miles until you got trapped under another fallen tree or the frigid river froze the life right out of you. I smoked one more joint, heaved my pack onto my back and started to walk the plank. As I was getting up onto the log, I noticed a couple hikers had just arrived at the crossing on the other side of the river. Ladies. Maybe I was hallucinating. I turned up my music and started the dance. It was part balancing, part agility, part jumping. It wasn't pretty. ¾ of the way across, I found myself on one leg teetering back and forth over whitewater on both sides, trying to stabilize, regain balance. I caught sight of the ladies faces who wore stunned looks like they were watching a building burn to the ground. Just as it looked and felt like I was surely going in the drink, out of pure desperation, I pulled off an out of body ninja-like hop skip jump and somehow found myself back on dry land, standing next to two very real, *very* attractive ladies who were now smiling and clapping. I pushed pause. "That was one hell of a show," one of them said. "We just crawl across the logs."

I thought for a second, realized how much safer that would be.

Emma and Lauren were from LA, hiking the JMT from North to South. They had been out here through the rain days and were covered in dried mud. Their beauty had been illuminated by the sun. I packed a bowl, we got high together. We chatted for awhile and really 'hit it off'. They had just graduated from UCLA, 'set out to have an adventure' before they got caught up in the 'real world'. Emma was short, petite with blond hair, and was starting Law School at Stanford in the fall. Lauren was tall, thin with a bob of dark brown hair and rich olive skin. She had landed a job at a hedge fund in Manhattan that started at the end of the summer.

"We passed a mountain lake 10 minutes ago on the trail, we should go swimming," said Lauren.

We hiked to the lake, off the main trail a few hundred yards, down a narrow path, surrounded by a high pine forest, secluded.

"Let's go skinny dipping!" hollered Lauren as she stripped off her shorts and tank top on her way towards the water. Then off came her sports bra and panties. She launched off a rock into a deep pool. I looked at Emma, she smiled.

"What are you waiting for sunshine?" she said as she stripped off her shirt. Out popped her perky b-cups. She ran towards the water launching off the rock into the lake, losing the rest of her clothes along the way. I touched

the tree next to me to see if it was real, it seemed real.
Thank you John Muir.
"Looks like someone's a little excited!" yelled
Lauren. "Hurry up the water's greeeaaat!"
    I undressed, ran towards the lake and did a
cannonball off the rock into a deep pool. I surfaced, swam
over to where the girls were. The water was clear and still
as glass. Dark triangles hypnotized me from below. Before
I knew what was happening Lauren was wrapped around
me. She grabbed me with her hand and guided me inside
her. It was very tight. I slid in halfway. Then slowly
pushed in the rest of the way as I kissed her. She began to
bob up and down. She began to moan. I began to moan.
Just as Lauren was about to finish me off, Emma swam
over. "Don't hog him all to yourself!" Lauren slipped off
of me, unwrapped her legs and Emma backed up to me
rubbing up and down, then pushed me inside of her. I held
on and ripped away until I couldn't possibly hold on and
exploded inside of her. We lay on the small sandy beach in
the hot July sun, smoking bowls. Naked. Every hour or so
one of them would mount. A rodeo at 8000 ft. I lasted
longer and longer as the day wore on. The sun lazily dipped
below the high western ridge. Tall pines cast long shadows
across the lake. Twilight settled in. We decided to camp
on the beach. I found a flat spot, set up my tent. We
crawled in. I ate a cliff bar to try to regain some energy.
The girls ate some trail mix. We managed to fit in my 1
person sleeping bag, in my 2 person tent. It was *cozy.*
Then it began again. Finally, we passed out.
    I woke mid-morning when the tent started to heat
up from the rising sun. I lay there thinking back on the
night trying to piece it all together until the girls woke up.
We had one more '*roundabout*' before breakfast, jumped in
the lake, then I fired up the jet-boil, brewed coffee and
cooked up a bowl of oatmeal for the three of us. "Well
ladies, that was quite possibly the best night of my life."
Thank you John Muir, I thought.

"We're going to miss you sunshine! Too bad we aren't hiking the same direction!" said Lauren. "I will miss you too, more than you know, be safe out there girls." I told them as we hugged and walked in our separate directions. I hiked on.

According to my map I had 5-6 miles further along the floor of this canyon before I hit my first significant climb. My body felt depleted. I was working harder for the same result now. By early afternoon I had reached my first slope to climb. It rose 2000 ft into the pure blue sky, it wasn't straight up, but damn near. The trail curled back and forth through the pines around large outcropping rocks and boulders. Switchbacks to the top. I smoked a joint, ate a cliff bar, smoked another joint. I was ready. I started slow, trying to find my rhythm, my legs were jello. Those girls had taken my trail legs with them. Then the endorphins started flowing, I gained momentum. I could feel my heart pounding in my chest, it was working hard. Halfway up I stopped to drink water. I smoked another joint. I heaved my pack onto my back. I hiked on. The final 300 yards the trail straightened out. A steep incline to the top. I let it have everything. As I was nearing the top, I heard the deep rumble of thunder. I slowed for the last few steps over the crest of the summit and stopped dead in my tracks when I saw it. The western sky was a shade somewhere in between a dark navy blue, and black coffee with enormous heinous looking thunderheads billowing up into the atmosphere. Lightning flared soundlessly. Growing up in the mid-west I had seen many a thunderstorm barreling down on the great plains, but nothing like this *boomer*.

The air temperature had dropped significantly, a cool ominous breeze began to blow. I guess this was that storm they had been talking about, *they* being the hikers *hi-tailing* it frantically in the opposite direction towards the shelter at Glen Aulin base camp 25 miles south of my current location. I pulled out my map, there was about a mile of switchbacks dropping 2000 ft into the canyon

below. I had to get to a lower elevation before it hit. Up
here at 10,000 ft I might as well be a marshmallow on the
end of a god damn smore skewer. I blazed down the trail.
It wasn't as steep as the side I had just come up, but it
wound back and forth through the rock and pine and a fall
off the trail would be one hell of a tumble. I was *feeling* it.
All those chemicals that make you feel *alive* were flowing.
I wound back and forth lower and lower. I was cruising
now, my pack felt like it was full of pillows. Finally, the
trail began to flatten out. The wind was starting to blow
furiously. 40-50 mph gusts bent the trees like toothpicks.
The edge of the front was upon me. Suddenly a huge bolt
of lightning ripped across the sky, a few seconds went by,
then ***booooooooooooom***! The echo repeated through the
surrounding mountains. It sounded like a bullet train
hitting a giant gong. Signaling its arrival. This thing was
here, I needed to hunker down *now*! I noticed a mountain
lake with huge granite boulders scattered around its shore
off to my left. I knew being near water wasn't ideal but
using one of the boulders as a shield was my only hope. I
found a flat spot near one of the boulders, dropped my pack
and quickly began setting up my tent. The wind was
ripping so hard now it was everything I could do to keep
the Kelty from taking off like a kite and disappearing into
the dark sky. I managed to get the stakes pounded in deep,
then took a rope, threaded one end through the stake holes,
the other around a smaller boulder near the tent as a last
resort to help keep it from blowing away. Then I heard
another sound. I looked out at the lake, a wall of rain was
moving across it. I threw my pack into my limp tent, began
threading the poles through as the wall of moisture hit. I
was instantly soaked from head to toe. Another flash, then
almost immediately *crraaaaaaaaaaaaaaaaack*, a deafening
boom of thunder seemed to rattle the entire earth around
me. My ears were ringing. I managed to get the poles
threaded and propped up. The boulder was helping as a
windbreak, even so, the only thing keeping my tent on the

planet was the rope anchoring it to the boulders. One more look towards the lake, 10 foot whitecaps rolled across its surface. I dove into my tent. Then I did the only thing I had left to do. I smoked 5 consecutive bowls. The white haze was so thick, I couldn't see the other side of the two person tent. I pulled my music out, pushed play. The Kelty seemed to do a frantic dance, like it was having one continuous seizure. I tried to find a song that fit the movement. Every few minutes the music would be trumped by a thundering boom. It sounded like bombs were being dropped all around me. Suddenly one of the tent poles was ripped from its hole and half the tent collapsed. I immediately smoked five more bowls before the tent went airborn. Shortly after my 10th consecutive bowl I must have passed out. (This still amazes me). The next thing I remember was waking up to the sound of the songbirds singing their morning *post-storm tune*. What was left of my tent was completely collapsed on top of me. It took a minute to remember why that would be. O yes, of course, *the storm*. I had survived my first storm on the trail. I unzipped the door of my tent, crawled out of the soaked pile of nylon.

The storm had left its mark. A tall pine tree had fallen 25 ft to my left. Sticks, branches, various forest debris littered the muddy ground. The Kelty was a shredded soggy mess. The rain guard was ripped in half. Two of the tent poles were snapped. I took my pack and sleeping bag out of the tent, hung what I could on the boulders to dry. The lake was still, buttery smooth. A hot, blue California morning. I brewed coffee, filled my mug, and climbed up on a boulder. I cranked the *Valencia album (dj coldsmoke)* and danced on the flat top of the boulder overlooking the still mountain lake for an hour. It was surreal. The beauty and solitude, serene and inspiring. I climbed down, cooked oatmeal, scooping a large dollop of peanut butter on top. I packed the battered Kelty and whatever else hadn't blown away. I hiked on.

For the next several days the weather was sunny and *extremely* hot. I would climb roughly 2000 ft up a slope, over the ridge, then descend back down the other side through switchbacks to the canyon below. An ascent descent of one of these mountains would take half the day, only knocking off a mile or two. In canyons I was knocking off mile after mile stopping intermittently by the shade of the streams to smoke joints and filter water. The extreme heat and constant ascending descending was beginning to take its toll. My body was being pushed to its limit. I started to notice my heart beating ridiculously hard near the tops of ascents. I ran into two guys on horses riding south, otherwise I didn't see a soul. I hiked on.

Late evening I was descending a long canyon that fell gradually downhill. This was now my 10th day in the mountains and my thoughts had reached a depth and clarity that I had never before experienced. The magic was real.

A fast flowing stream braided alongside the trail. I was *toast*, looking for a spot to set up camp. I rounded a corner and well below me, a few miles down the trail a lake came into view. Mountains seemed to surround the lake on all sides except the side I was approaching from. I could see the water glistening in the evening sunlight. A light haze hung on the long blue dusk. I continued descending lower, lower, eventually into a thick forest. The trail came to a fork. I took the trail towards the lake. The narrow path curled through the forest. After walking for a quarter mile I walked out onto a white sand beach. The other three sides surrounding the lake where sheer cliffs that turned into steep slopes up to a high ridge-line 1500 ft above the calm water. An amphitheater. I stood on the beach in awe. It was the most enchanting place I'd ever been. I wondered if this was the mythical lake that Ansel Adams had famously never photographed because of its rare magical beauty (it was). I walked across the soft pink and orange sand, set up camp on the far side of the beach, halfway between the water and the trees. I managed to tape the broken tent poles together with hockey tape that I found buried deep in my pack, my tent sagged a bit more than normal but considering what it had been through, I was just glad it was still usable.

I awoke to the motionless morning lake of glass. A brown trout jumped as I popped my head out to exhale my first puff of smoke of the day. My body was hurting. The miles were starting to take their toll. I could feel that I wasn't taking in enough calories. I fired up the jet-boil, brewed coffee and cooked an extra serving of oatmeal with two scoops of peanut butter on top. I ate my breakfast sitting in the soft shaded sand. Once again there wasn't a cloud in the sky and it was going to be a *heater*. Part of me wanted to stay at this enchanted lake for the day, rest, and continue on tomorrow but I still had forty some miles to go until the re-supply. I was barely half-way. I needed to keep moving. As I was finishing my coffee I studied my trail maps. Several large climbs lay ahead over the next 15 miles, I was in for one hell of a day. I found a lake 15 miles away, made that my goal for the day. I had been putting in some solid days but after studying my maps and doing some rough calculations, I realized it was going to be *very* tight with food. I packed my battered tent. Filtered water from the lake, filling my canteen. I stood on the beach soaking up the magic. I imagined John Muir, Ansel Adams standing on this beach all those years ago. After ripping two consecutive joints, I turned and walked towards the woods. I hiked on.

The blistering sun was heating up the day. I crossed a trickling stream, then started climbing. It was gradual to begin with, then steadily got steeper as I climbed out of the shaded forest of the canyon towards the high, distant ridge-line. I put my head down, fell into the trail trance. By mid-morning the merciless sun beat down relentlessly on me as I neared the top of the first ridge of the day. I forced myself to keep drinking water even though I wasn't thirsty.

I could feel my heart pounding like a jackhammer in my chest as I climbed.

    I hiked on. Grinding forward through mid-day, then afternoon, the trail and sun beating the fuck out of me simultaneously. Up over a tall ridge, across a mountain pass, then back down into another deep canyon. Then back up again. By early evening the sun was finally starting to relent a bit as I hobbled deliriously along a gurgling stream. I came across a few flat, cleared off spots along the creek with the remnants of a campfire between them. These were the designated 'camps' along the trail. I put down my pack, pulled out my trail maps to try to figure out where I was. I was able to locate the camp I was at and it presented me with a dilemma. The next camp was 5 more miles, up and over a mountain. I had 3-4 hours of daylight left. If I didn't make it before dark, I would be in steep treacherous terrain, trying to find the camp in the dark. I filtered water from the cold stream, smoked a joint while I contemplated. I hiked on.

    Soon the trail edged upwards, starting to gain elevation. I continued to grind towards the slowly darkening sky, starting to feel a second wind. A race against the sun. It was falling faster than I was rising. The trail became so steep that it turned into switchbacks winding back and forth among the pine and rock. A 1000 ft tumble through rocks and trees. This was going to be a *cluster-fuck* in the dark! I reached a rollover. A false summit. The trail flattened out for 500 ft, then climbed another 500 ft up a steep slope. I walked over the crest of the ridge as the sun was disappearing. Forty-five minutes of twilight left at most. I hiked on, ripping down the side of the mountain. Slipping, sliding, dodging rocks, grabbing trees to avoid falling over the edge into the abyss. Back and forth I wound lower and lower. The switchbacks seemed endless. As the last of the light was snuffed out, I dropped my pack, dug around for my headlamp. I found it buried deep in the bottom. I turned the light on, heaved my pack on my shoulders and continued into the pitch-black night. By this point I had been hiking for almost fifteen hours. I was delirious. My legs were jello. I was too tired to be scared, too tired to care anymore. All I could do was put one foot in front of the other. I hiked on.

Suddenly my foot caught on a branch and I tripped forward falling hard on the rocky trail. The sharp jagged rocks sliced open my skin like a dull chef's blade. I could feel the blood running down my arms and legs. I rolled over, lay there on my back, my headlamp pointing up into the clear, silent, star filled sky. An electric kite. It was magnificent. More stars than I had ever seen in my life littered the pure black backdrop. I rolled onto my stomach, pushed myself to my knees. It took every ounce of strength I had left. As I lifted my head up looking down the trail, the light illuminated two beady eyes, 15 ft away, staring back at me. They were too far off the ground to be a raccoon. Too low to be a deer, elk or moose. Too small to be a bear. My best guess was a god damn cougar. A large shot of adrenaline shot through my veins. What in the *lively fuck* was the protocol for cougars? Ring a bell? Play dead? Bake them a cake and sing a song? I had no clue. Then came the low grotesque growl. I didn't have a gun. I'd emptied my bear spray on the *lower east side mugger*. I couldn't go back the way I'd come, I had no energy to climb back up this damn mountain. The Mexican standoff lasted several minutes. Suddenly, in an impulsive, out of body-like experience, I picked up a large rock and hurled it in the direction of the cat as I closed my eyes and charged down the trail. I braced. The impact never came. I opened my eyes, the cat was gone. Vanished into the night. The crazy deranged hiker routine was apparently the answer I was looking for. Probably thought I was rabid.

I continued to stumble deliriously down the trail, pushed on by the surge of adrenaline from the encounter. After another hour of switchbacks, the trail began to flatten out and soon I came upon the shore of a lake. The water glistened in the silver light of the moon. A cold breeze blew across the lake, chilling my sweat drenched clothes to the bone. The night-time temps were near freezing up at these higher elevations. I needed to get in my bag as soon as possible. I pulled out my map to see where on the lake the camp was located. Southwest corner. I was in the southeast corner. I walked west along the shoreline for another hour. Halfway across I was stopped by a barb-wire fence with a gate made from small logs. In my delirious state I nearly walked into it. A small sign on the gate said it was an animal fence. To keep the big game out. It took me ten minutes to get the latch unstuck and gate opened. Finally, I was able to get it open and pass through. The moon hung high in the sky, almost full. I walked through woods on the southern shore of the lake. Finally, I walked into a small clearing on the edge of the lake, a small red tent sat near the shore. I was covered in blood, dirt, mud, I could barely walk my legs were so tired. I hadn't eaten since 3 or 4 o'clock, having started rationing my dwindling cliff bars. After some struggle, I managed to get my hockey taped tent to stand, albeit with a slight lean and a bit of a droop. I was shivering violently now. I threw my pack in my tent, crawled in, and climbed into my sleeping bag zipping it over my head. I quickly drifted off to sleep to the soothing sound of waves lapping against the shore.

I awoke shivering at dawn. I had wriggled partially out of my sleeping bag. It was *freezing*. It felt like I had been beaten by an angry mob. My stomach growled furiously. Slowly but surely the previous night came back to me. I took a couple sips from my water bottle, entombed in cold frost. I began to shiver uncontrollably. I found my jet-boil, fired it up and brewed a bowl of steaming oatmeal, lots of peanut butter on top. I ate. I smoked 4 bowls. I passed out.

I awoke again around eleven. It was now easily 90 degrees in my tent. I gulped down my water, crawled out of my tent into another hot, cloudless day. The lake shimmered and sparkled in the sun. The red tent still sat by the lake, but I didn't see anyone around. I surveyed the damage to my body, the fronts of my arms and legs were ripped to shreds and covered in dried dark red/black blood.

The lake fed a stream that flowed into a deep canyon. I walked across the camp, climbed onto a boulder to get a better view. I could see small waterfalls that fell into deep pools just beyond the camp. I decided to go for a swim below the waterfall. I stripped down to my boxers and headed for the waterfalls. I gingerly made my way across the top of the shallow pools above the falls and found a perch on a dry rock near the edge. The gently flowing water dropped 15 ft into a deep, clear pool. I jumped.

The ice cold water shocked some life back into my system. I surfaced, found my way to the edge, circled back to make the jump three more times. I felt like a kid again. I lingered on the edge of the deep pool scrubbing the blood from my arms and legs. When I got back to camp there was a woman sitting on the shore, looking out at the lake. She turned around just as I was nearing the tents. My heart skipped a beat. A trail angel. She was stunningly beautiful. She had shoulder length light brown-blond hair. A rich midsummer tan. She was short, petite, maybe 5'4". She was barefoot, wore skintight black yoga shorts and a light blue sports bra. She looked mid-twenties. Her body was straight out of SI swimsuit edition. She smiled when she saw me. I smiled back, walked over to say hi forgetting that I was only wearing boxers until I was almost to her. As I got closer our eye's met and I realized I couldn't breathe. They were a stony blue with a hint of green, soft, kind, full of a mixture of sadness and passion.

"Hi I'm Jack." I managed to say. She smiled wider and let out a cute laugh.

"I'm Mia, nice to meet you Jack."

I sat down next to her in the sand and we chatted all afternoon overlooking the lake. Her story was fascinating.

Mia was 27, she was an artist originally from Portland. She had gone to school at Stanford on a full art scholarship but dropped out after 2 years. She had then moved to New York City to try to live her dream fully supporting herself selling her paintings. She spent two years grinding it out living on next to nothing in hole in the wall apartments, working shitty restaurant jobs to eek by, all the while spending every spare minute painting, filling her apartment with paintings. She tried to get her foot into gallery after gallery with no success. Except for the odd sale for a few hundred dollars she couldn't sell her work. After years of struggling she was on the verge of giving up, moving back to Portland when one day, she was painting by the lake in Central Park. A man approached her, offered to buy the painting she was working on for 3,000$ cash, on one condition. She had to go out for dinner with him as well. He was older than her, but not old, maybe 31. Very well dressed, he seemed fairly normal. That's 3 months rent, I can get through one dinner with this suit for 3 grand, she reasoned. Shortly after she agreed, his driver and car drove up. Long story short, she said, it was the first of many dinners. They fell in love. Ian came from an extremely wealthy east coast family, had graduated from Yale and continued the family tradition on Wall Street. He was sweet and smart and interesting in the beginning. Shortly after they began dating, Ian had offered to rent out a gallery space in mid-town Manhattan so she could put on an exhibition featuring her stockpile of paintings. It took a U-haul to get all the paintings to the gallery. Ian invited the upper echelon of New York society, the real old money crowd. In one night Mia sold every last painting she had brought... for *4 million dollars*. In one night she had gone from an unknown, broke waitress, with a room full of paintings, to a multi-millionaire and now one of the most sought after new artists in Manhattan. The commissions came flooding in and for the next several months she barely left her upper east side loft trying to keep up with demand.

The money was rolling in. When she wasn't painting she was partying. Drugs, booze, paint, sex, *rock and roll.* Repeat. The wave lasted for a year and finally it all blew up. She had come home to find Ian in bed with 3 high end escorts one night. The more she experienced and learned about the art world of New York City, and the "fake lame ass rich fucks" that were buying her art, the more disillusioned she became.

One cold spring day much unlike the rest, she packed a suitcase, bought a one way plane ticket for Indonesia, and never looked back. She had been traveling the world for a year. Bali, Bangkok, Sydney, Oslo, Rome, Paris, Machu Pichu, Cali (Columbia), Tangier, Fiji, London, Maui, and now had come out to the trail to try to find herself again. I was completely mesmerized, fascinated by her story, by her. She had this kindness, this innocence about her, also a sadness, brokenness. She asked about my story. I sat in silence looking out at the water. "Jack it's ok if..." I hadn't told anyone that story for a very long time, making up some run of the mill bland story when people asked, but for some reason I trusted her. *I told her all of it.*

Death had woven itself deep into the fabric of my life from early on. My mother, a gifted painter, died during the childbirth of my younger brother Eddie when I was four. My Father, a jazz musician and *hopeless junkie,* was incapacitated by grief, cranked up the dope, died of an overdose a year later. They were gone before I was old enough to remember much about them and I knew them mostly from stories. I'd been raised by my grandparents. Wonderful hardy-hardworking mid-western folks. My grandfather was a WWII war hero, a recipient of the Bronze Star for saving his entire platoon. He had taken out a Japanese tank that was wreaking havoc on them by modifying a long range mortar launcher, tipping it on its side, as the story goes, (and I didn't hear it from him, he never told a soul about the medal, not even his wife), he blew that tank damn near back to Tokyo. He had spent the better part of 2 years landing on beaches in the South Pacific, at one point going 140 days and nights in a row without a break from front-line combat. I don't know who he was when he left for the War, but when he came back he was *unbreakable*, overpowered any hardship life hurled at him like it was nothing at all. We called him the *war-horse*. To this day he's the toughest man I've ever met. He once told me the War was why he believed in God, said the likelihood of him surviving what he survived over there was less than zero without some sort of divine intercession. My Grandmother was the life of every party, baked the best apple pie in the tri-state. My grandparents both passed away within the same year when I was 14 and my brother was 10. Eddie was my only family left and best friend in the world.

Then one cold autumn day a year after we had been put in foster care, Eddie passed out in the front yard. They rushed him to the hospital. After several days of tests they determined he had leukemia. Eddie passed 7 months later. The last two, I slept on the floor in his hospital room. I held his hand until the end, my heart slowly shattered as he slipped away.

The day after Eddie passed, I packed my suitcase and hit the road. I was propelled through the fog of grief by pain, day after day, stumbling forward into the lonely world wishing I would *disappear*. Those years made me *hard as fuck*, ready as I could be for the even rougher road that lay ahead.

When I was 18 I found *hope* when I met Claire. Claire became my family. She was too cool, like a cross between Mary Poppins and Billy Holiday. Blue eyes with no bottoms like the sea. The romance of her hair. Nights full of blue-haze. I liked the way she cussed, she cussed with great beauty. She had an untouchable charisma. Claire softened me, *loved* me, brought out the joy in me that had been buried so deep for so long. We had each other and that was enough. *More* than enough, we were in *love*. I've never met anyone like her before or since.

It was like a dream, and like in dreams, I didn't get to stay. Two years later it was the night before Thanksgiving, Claire had set out on her bike to the market an hour before to get a few last minute things for our feast the following day when I got the call. I fell to my knees, curled up in the fetal position on the kitchen floor. I couldn't move for three days. A truck had run a red light. Claire was *dead*.

Losing Claire finally broke me. For the next several years the wheels completely fell off. I smoked, snorted, shot-up, and drank myself into *absolute oblivion*.

I woke up in the San Francisco Bay. I woke up under a bridge in Vancouver. I woke up in Denver County Jail, one shoe missing (apparently there had been a 'foot-chase'). I woke up on railroad tracks in the deep woods of northern MN, both shoes, shirt gone. I woke up in the Oslo airport. I woke up in a canal in Amsterdam. I woke up bouncing across a choppy Norwegian fjord in a jet-boat. I woke up in a pool of blood, in an alley in the heart of Marseilles, everything missing. I woke up in various towns along the west coast of France, on various beaches along the east coast of Italy. I woke up in a fountain in the town center of Milan wearing nothing but goggles, a snorkel, and a pair of water wings, *both popped*. I had diving fins on my feet, one looked like it was partially melted, the other had an imprint of a shark's jaw missing from the top left corner. I paddled to the edge of the fountain, asked a homeless man dangling his feet in the water what day it was. Upon hearing his answer, I realized my last coherent memory was three-five weeks prior. I woke up on a bench in Paris. I woke up in a 1987 Dodge Dart parked at the base of the Great Pyramid, hands handcuffed to the steering-wheel. I woke up on a rooftop in Tangier wearing nothing but a hash pipe necklace and water shoes. I woke up in the hull of the Queen Mary II. I woke up on a skiff off the southwest coast of Cuba, fishing rod duck-taped to my hand, line in water, fish on. I woke up in Key West Florida, halfway across the 7 mile bridge. I woke up...

As hard as I tried not to, wished I wouldn't, somehow I continued to wake up day after day, and day after day, the pain was right there with me.

I had gotten hooked on reading as a way to escape reality at some point along the way. I read a book a day for years. In the wake of Claire's death, I began writing. The words flowed from the dark ether. *It helped to get them out.* Deep in a drug-fueled haze I pounded away at my typewriter nightly, waking amongst a pile of pages each morning. After a year I had completed my first novel. It was too personal, and I was so fucked up when I wrote it, I published it under an obscure pen name when I was 21 years old. Didn't tell a soul about it. Through a strange sequence of unlikely events the book went viral. Apparently hit some sort of nerve. Sold like hotcakes. Like a fart in the wind, I had been living off the royalties ever since, which in recent years had begun to dwindle. Hadn't written a word since, *I'd been skiing.*

One frigid December night after getting a whole next level of loaded, in a complete blackout, fate intervened as I stumbled onto a bus headed *west.* When I woke the next morning we were rolling through the Montana mountains. I stumbled off in Bozeman. Big Sky country. I was home. The snow-capped peaks got me clean. Rather, skiing was my new drug of choice. *Addiction in disguise.* Skiing was my escape from the 'world'. Skiing kept me in the moment. In the mountains, I could see life crystal clear. I became a ski bum in a cold mountain town, skiing 120 days a year. Hiking and biking the rest. *Fuck it.*

Well, except when I was injured. Over the years the mountains beat me to a pulp. I fell three times in no fall zones. Normally, you only get one fall in a no fall zone, I was lucky. I shattered my legs, arms, a plethora of other bones I can't name. Doctors told me I would never walk again. They told me I certainly wouldn't ski again. I did. I was *lucky*. One clear, cold January day, on my morning bike ride to the coffee shop I hitchhiked up to the mountain from, I was hit by a truck going 45 mph at the intersection of Black and Garfield. When the snow settled, the truck was totaled, the hood crumpled up like an accordion. My bicycle was missing the rubber grip on the right handlebar, I picked it out of the snow, slipped it back on. *Lucky.* Twice, I had found myself miles in the deep backcountry, somewhere between life and death, my only chance at survival being if a helicopter showed up out of the clear blue sky. It had. *Twice.* **Lucky.**

As I got older, despite my best efforts, I simply could not escape my tortured mind. Then one day, seemingly out of the blue, the migraines settled in, took hold of me, pulling me down into the dark, cold depths of constant suffering. Now I had shattered bones, I'd been beaten like a pinata by the mountains. I'd been hit by a goddamn truck. That pain was childs-play. This was different, this pain wrapped around my head like a vice-grip, clamped down mercilessly, day after day, month after month, year after year, and slowly snuffed the will to live right out of me. Finally, one day, as I stood atop a high Montana peak, I had an epiphany that hit me like a spring avalanche that had ripped to the ground. *My hand was played.* Time to retire, fold the tent. *I didn't want to be here anymore.* More than that, I just wanted the pain to *finally* be gone.

I decided I would dust off the needle and spoon, blast off to join the rest of them.

But first, I would go on a trip. A farewell tour. One last marathon stunt ride. *One for the books.* Hop on the torpedo, launch into the great beyond, hold the *lively fuck* on.

I packed a backpack with a few pair of clothes, two of my favorite books, and as much weed as I could possibly fit. I put all my shit out on the curb with a *free* sign, told my landlord, *tough tittie*, bought a multi-city plane ticket and lit the fuse.

I was out here in the California wilderness, hoping the trail would either kill me or make me want to live again.

I glanced over at Mia to see if she was still listening. Our eyes met again. Two kindred spirits sitting on the beach of a mountain lake at 10,000 feet. Fifty miles from the nearest hint of civilization. *Thank you John Muir.*

We sat talking on that beach until the sun began setting and the cool breeze off the lake turned cold. We built a small campfire. I cooked oatmeal, Mia warmed up soup. We had a picnic under the wine-colored sky. After dinner, Mia smiled at me, said she had a surprise. She went into her tent, returning with marshmallows, graham crackers, chocolate. "I've been saving them until I had someone to share them with." We sat roasting smores & bowls. Telling stories, laughing. Finally, it was too cold to stay out any longer. We walked towards the tents.

"What the fuck happened to your tent?" she asked.

"That storm a couple nights ago beat it up pretty good. Weren't you out in it?"

"I was up by lake Dorothy, I found a small cave cut into a cliff on the south shore of the lake and set up my tent in it. I could barely tell it was raining back in there."

I unzipped my tent, began to crawl in..."Well if you get cold...the doors always open over here at the hockey-tape shack...zippers broken." She smiled, without saying anything... it looked like she was thinking about it. We crawled into our tents. It was quiet. The only sounds were the gentle waves lapping against the shore and the distant song of a coyote. I lay there for a half hour, nowhere near sleep. Then as if I was dreaming Mia crawled through the door of my tent. Squeezed in the bag with me.

"It's cold and lonely over there." was all she said.

"I'm glad you're here," was all I could get out.

She snuggled up against my body, I put my arm around her. Then she rolled over and we were face to face. I kissed her lightly at first, she kissed me back. Then it was mayhem. She ripped my boxers off, I leaned up on my knees and slipped off her yoga shorts and bra. I went down on her, went to work with my tongue. She was already very wet, moaning, gently pulling my hair. When it seemed she couldn't take anymore I worked my way up her body lingering on her hard nipples on the way to her mouth. As we kissed, her hand gently grabbed me and guided me inside her. I slowly worked my way all the way in. She pulled me down on top of her as I started slowly. I sped up and she moaned. Then I slowed again, tried the change up. I felt like I was trying out for the *New York Yankees*!

"You feel sooooo good inside me." she whispered in my ear as she lightly bit it.

I gained confidence, had the momentum, I picked up speed. On and on I went, I couldn't believe it!

"Fuck me like it's the last night of our *liiiiiives*" she moaned desperately as she arched her back, kicking her feet way up in the air. *Thank you John Muir! I thought.*

I leaned back up on my arms, gave her everything I had. I could sense she was close, I hung on. We both went into orbit as I leaned in and kissed her hard. Both of us shuddered and shook, she pulled me back down on top of her. We lay there for several minutes, breathing hard. I was still inside her. Time stopped. I could die happy. I rolled off. *I think I had made the team.*

I woke early again. Mia was cuddled up, still sleeping. I could see my breath, we were warm together in the bag. I fell back asleep. I woke again a couple hours later and Mia was awake, still cuddled up against me. We both smiled when our eye's met. "That was a good night."

"Yes it was." she said with a smile.

We crawled out of the tent, still naked. I ran for the lake, into the water until it got too deep and pulled me under. When I surfaced Mia was running for the water.

Those beautiful c-cups bouncing in the gentle morning light. We swam as long as we could take the frigid water, then both walked back to the tents, dressed. I began brewing up a bowl of oatmeal.

I needed to get back on the trail today. I had enough food for a day and a half. I had 30 miles with 6,000 ft of elevation change between me and the next re-supply. My back was against the wall. I studied my map as I was cooking breakfast, it soon became clear it was going to take a small miracle. As I was studying my map I also noticed that Dorothy Lake was north of my current position 10 miles. The question that had been bothering me since I awoke with Mia in my arms had been answered. Mia was hiking South. My heart immediately sank. As I thought about it more I realized it was for the best. We had both come out here alone, to face the trail alone, to be shaped by the trail alone. Mia emerged from her tent in her hiking apparel, looking even more beautiful than the day before. She sat next to me on the beach, I put my arm around her and pulled her in tight, kissing her on the top of her head.

"I think we should just live here on this lake forever, just you and me, living off the land."

"That sounds lovely" she said, "but I think we both know we would last about a week before this place finished us off."

"Oh I doubt we'd last that long... I'm going to be running on *fumes* rolling into the next checkpoint, if I make it." There was a long pause. "You need to keep hiking south, don't you?" I asked her quietly. There was a silence and then she turned and nodded as a tear slid down her cheek.

"And you need to keep hiking north don't you?"

I nodded, hugging her tighter.

"How far are you going?" she asked.

"Until the wheels fall off. I've got maps for 1000 miles but I doubt it will take that long... you?"

"As long as it takes."

We sat looking out at the lake in silence holding each other, trying to delay the inevitable. Finally, she sensed it was time. We packed up our tents, organized our packs and came together for one more embrace.

"I'm very happy I met you." I said as we hugged. I handed her the small slip of paper I had written my e-mail on, her stone blue eyes welled up with tears. I turned to walk north. I made it ten feet, dropped my pack, ran back to her kissing her, hugging her tight, lifting her off the ground. I set her back down, turned, and never looked back.

I began grinding into the furnace of a day. According to my maps the trail steadily gained elevation for the next 10 miles up to lake Dorothy, right on the border of Yosemite. I would need to make it well past that if I was going to have any chance at reaching the re-supply tomorrow. My food would be gone tomorrow mid-day. My back was against the wall. This wilderness was starting to sink its teeth into me, going in for the kill. The heat and miles and lack of calories continued to wear my body down through the mid-day heat. I came upon Lake Dorothy sometime in the afternoon. A big dark blue lake with jagged peaks guarding its southern shore. Snow still clung to the tops of their peaks. Suddenly, I felt lightheaded and dizzy. I went down to my knees to keep from toppling off the trail into the woods. I remembered looking down from the plane, seeing the mid-July snow covered peaks, thinking how rugged, harsh, dangerous it must be down there. *It had brought me to my knees.* According to my map I was up over 11,000 ft now. Maybe it was the altitude, maybe it was the lack of food, whatever was wrong, my body was shutting down. I pushed myself back up onto my feet and staggered down a path to the waterfront to filter some cold lake water. I dug in my pack for my steri-pen which was what I depended on to purify water. I frantically dug around in the top pocket of my pack. It was my lifeline to clean water. It wasn't there.

When was the last time I had used it? I remembered
filtering water from a stream an hour back on the trail. I
had no choice but to go back to try to find it. I left my pack
by the lake, taking only my water-bottle with what little
purified water was left in it, and headed back south. I
walked along the trail searching the ground. Three more
dizzy spells hit me in a matter of 15 minutes but I managed
to stay on my feet. Finally, I made it back to the spot by
the stream. I searched everywhere for 20 minutes.
Nothing. It simply wasn't here. I was just going to have to
drink the water straight out of the streams. *Fuck it.*

I staggered uphill an hour back to Lake Dorothy.
As I approached my pack I noticed the hood of my rain
jacket was hanging lower than normal. I reached in, resting
in the bottom of my hood was my steri-pen. It was like it
had magically appeared from thin air. *Lucky.* I quickly
purified and drank a liter of water, then refilled one to bring
with. I hiked on. Staggering down the trail. Lightheaded,
dizzy. I put one foot in front the other. Full grind. I was at
that point now. But for some odd reason I wasn't worried.
I loved this place. The end of yourself. The end of the
line. I didn't care what happened, I was *free.* I made it past
the shores of lake Dorothy and the trail started to work
upwards again to the crest of the mountain pass a half mile
ahead. As I ground my way up the slope I heard the
hollow, rythmic thump thump thump of a helicopter. I
knew that sound anywhere. As I reached the top of the
crest, there it was. A black helicopter hovering 100 ft off
the ground, a basket slowly lowering. A hiker was on the
ground awaiting the basket. It reached him on the ground,
he hopped in the basket and was lifted back up to the
helicopter as it flew away to the north. I noticed a wooden
sign on the side of the trail. Now leaving Yosemite
National Park. I pulled out my maps to check my location.
I'd hiked 10 miles today. I needed to grind out another 10
to be in reach of the highway I could hitchhike to the re-
supply from tomorrow. It was around 5 in the evening, the

steri-pen debacle had wasted two hours. I took another precious bite of cliff bar. I hiked on.

The trail led me gradually down into another canyon floor. The heat of the day was past now. I drifted into the trail trance, started pounding out miles. The landscape changed, much less granite, a thick pine and redwood forest. At some point I heard a rattlesnake warning his presence, but never saw him. I hiked on.

As dusk settled in, I was crossing a stream deep in a canyon, an old tent caught my eye. It was 30 ft off the trail, in the dark, shadow filled woods. It was no backpackers tent. It was much bigger, more permanent, made from old heavy canvas. I didn't see anyone around it. A fire smoldered outside the door. The forest was eerily silent. I heard a twig snap. I whirled around and a very old man was standing on the path ten feet behind me. He was short, nothing but skin and bone, had a gray beard, bald head. His sunken crazed eyes were staring at me. His clothes were damn near rags. In his right hand, he held a nearly empty bottle of whiskey, a tall hiking staff in his left. His belt had a machete hanging from it. He wasn't smiling. His cold stare sent a chill through my body. He started pounding the staff on the ground as he quickly walked towards me. I took off running. After about a mile I was completely gassed and finally slowed, checked behind. He was gone. Who the fuck was *that* guy? I was still miles from the nearest road. He looked like he had lived out here for years. Damn, if the bears or bobcats didn't finish you off, the blitzed hermits might. *Fuck me.* I hiked on.

Soon it was dark. I staggered down the trail by the light of the moon for hours in a trance. One foot in front of the other. I didn't stop to eat, I didn't stop to drink, didn't stop to smoke. I staggered forward, delirious. It felt like a dream. The bright full moon hung high in the sky. The crickets chanted, otherwise it was silent. The trail began to work back uphill and I could see the outline of a high ridge-line on the dark horizon. The final climb to the highway. I pulled out my map. I was approximately 7 miles from the elusive road. I had been hiking for 16 hours, almost 23 miles. The last spot to camp was about a mile away from my current location. Beyond that you would be on the steep exposed mountain until the road. Over the next mile I contemplated whether to continue through the night, go for the highway without stopping to sleep. Suddenly, I became extremely dizzy and fell backwards nearly smacking my head on a large boulder on the side of the trail. The decision was made, I would camp here. I rolled out my sleeping pad on the trail, drank a few big gulps of water, forced down a scoop of peanut butter and crawled into my sleeping bag. I lay there looking up into the silence of the stars.

I woke shivering at dawn. The eastern sky had shapes of light in it behind puzzle pieces of clouds. It felt like I had been hit by a bus. I had a terrible headache and everything hurt.

I packed up my sleeping bag and mat, scooped the last of my peanut butter into my mouth, forcing it down with a few gulps of water. I walked down to the nearby stream, filtered and drank a full liter of water. Then filtered another, smoked two joints to ease the pain and began down the trail. Willing one foot in front of the other. After a quarter mile I walked out of the shaded forest and began the steep treeless slope already heating up from the quickly rising morning sun. According to my tattered map, I was up near 12,000 ft and I could feel the effects of the thin air not helping my plight. The sun was relentless. It felt like I was being *baked* alive. Halfway up the steep, rocky, sun scorched slope, a wave of dizziness rushed over me. My arms and legs became heavy, I fell to my knees, threw up, and again. Then came the tightness in my chest, as if a hand was squeezing my heart, trying to pop it like a water balloon. *The wheels had finally fallen off.* I sat leaned against a boulder, lit up a joint.

A few years back I'd been skiing in the Northern Bridgers when the same feeling overtook me. Tightness in my chest, then my arms and legs became very heavy, then I'd collapsed and blacked out. The friend I had been skiing with, *a mountain goat of a man*, had been able to get to the top of the ridge-line, miraculously he found cell service, ordered up the 'ice-cream truck'. They were over the top of us in 7 minutes, had managed to drop down for a 'hot load' through the snowy skies and get me to the ER. The doctors said my heart had suffered similar damage to a heart attack, but I hadn't had a heart attack. It took three more days of tests for them to determine that I had pericarditis, an inflammation of the lining around the heart. Not necessarily a serious condition if it isn't irritated past a certain point, the heart is able to function normally and eventually the inflammation goes away. However if you stress it enough, which apparently I had done, it can become so inflamed that it clamps down on the heart like a straight jacket. Either kills you outright, or if your heart is strong enough to withstand the pressure, it is able to continue to pump enough blood to keep you alive. They kept me in the ICU for a week. Finally, after a week in the hospital they filled a bag with medications, let me loose. After reading the endless lists of potential side effects, I'd tossed them. Stuck to my 10 joints a day routine, hoped for the best, or worst, I didn't want anything in between. Slowly but surely my health returned. For the first month, I felt 80, couldn't walk around the block. Month two I began biking. Six months later I was skiing, a year later I felt normal again.

I began this *foray* into the wilderness nearly two years after that debacle, figured my heart was tip top. Apparently, it couldn't cut the mustard. The tightness in my chest worsened. It felt like a fist was squeezing my heart. Another wave of lightheaded dizziness hit me. I went down to my knees, then threw up everything in my stomach. It didn't take long to calculate just how *fucked* I was. I looked down the trail. It wound endlessly upwards for the next 7 miles. Up the unprotected sun scorched mountain. I knew I would never make it.

My only option was to get off this mountain, to a lower elevation. Into the shade of the forest, near the stream. Wait. I got back to my feet and started gingerly walking down the steep slope. I threw up three more times before I made it to the trees. Water and bile. I found a shaded spot off the trail, near the stream, collapsed. I fished the flipper out of my pack and pressed the power button to turn it on. Just to make sure by some strange aligning of the stars I didn't have service. The ancient flip phone fired up, the main screen indicated it was searching for service. It also indicated the date was 14 days ago. I pushed the power button. The wait began. I had seen 3 people in the past week, including the crazed hermit. I continued sipping water. It continued coming back up. It was well over 90 in the shade. Hours went by, the mid-day heat giving way to the afternoon heat. Screeching calls of vultures echoed around the walls of the canyon. Signaling to the coyotes a future meal was near. I lay there, suffering, starting to hope my body would just give out.

Hours passed. Dusty clockless hours. I drifted in and out. I heard voices coming down the trail. One of them spotted me by the stream. A biology professor, five students. They were on day one of a 3 day trip to a remote backcountry lake to take samples for a research project. I asked if they by chance had a satellite phone.

"You'd have to be *crazy* to be out here without one!" Susan, the professor, said.

"Yes."

Susan was mid-forties, had green eyes, long brown hair, looked like a mom. "Anne, you've got the phone right?" A nerdy looking girl with short black hair and big glasses fished a phone from her pack and began punching buttons. Five minutes passed. *'Chopper is on the way, 45 min eta. wave bright colors when overhead.'*

As we waited, Susan, Anne, Ethan, John, and Mariah took care of me. Susan insisted I eat some of her homemade banana bread, had to get something in my stomach, she said. They gave me a bottle of Gatorade to drink. Before long we heard the thump thump thump of the chopper and spotted it approaching us from the north. It was a different helicopter than I had seen the day before. Brown with a Sheriffs emblem on the side. As it neared us Susan and the students started waving shirts. The heli hovered over the top of us, 200 ft above the trees. There seemed to be a problem. They hovered over the top of us again, yelling something at us with a megaphone. It was impossible to know what they were saying over the roar of the engine and rotors. They flew back to the northeast, soon disappearing out of sight. "Must be having trouble finding a spot to land," said Susan.

We waited. Another hour went by, the afternoon burned through into evening. We waited. Susan poured me Gatorade. "Electrolytes," she said, "got to get those electrolytes back in you." We waited.

We heard another helicopter approaching. This one was much smaller. It hovered over the top of us for a few minutes, then began descending to a spot 200 yards away, out of the trees, at the base of the steep slope. The wind from its rotors whipped up dirt, dust, and leaves. The roar of the engine blotted out all other sound. It landed, powered down. The pilot and medic ran toward us armed with a stretcher and large first aid bag. The pilot, George, wore a flight suit, aviator sunglasses, crew cut hair and had a cool, calm demeanor - just another day at the office.

"We had a hell of a time getting on the ground out here, first bird was just too big, no chance."

Brad, the medic, was tall, with red blond hair, stressed, intense and focused. He frantically went to work, checking vitals, asking his list of questions, hooking me up to a portable ekg machine. Whatever his machine told him caused his eyes to bulge. He grabbed a syringe from his bag, gave me a shot in the arm, then looked at George. "We've got to get him to Tahoe now!" he said, trying, failing to sound calm. "George, fire up the bird! This is a hot load!"

I had heard the term 'hot load' before and while it didn't sound great, I knew it was better than a 'cold load'. I was able to shimmy onto the stretcher. Brad, Susan, and all 5 students lifted me up and navigated the uneven terrain across the stream, up to the heli. "Thank you for helping me!" I yelled over the roar of the rotors.

George already had the engine started, the blast of wind and noise from the engine and rotors was overpowering. The stretcher fit to the side of the pilot's seat, Brad's seat was directly behind the pilot. Brad put a headset on me and told me I could sit up if I wanted. I did. We lifted off. About the same time, whatever Brad had shot into my arm started to take effect and a warm floating sensation moved from the backs of my legs up my spine to the back of my neck, then all over. We have *liftoff*. We flew straight up until we were above the trees, then flew north. Brad carefully monitored my vitals, told me to lay back down if I felt lightheaded or dizzy. I felt *high*. Whatever he had shot me up with was trumping everything else. As we flew over the rugged mountainous terrain I pointed out the highway that I needed to make it to.

"Never would have made it," said George "it was damn near straight up all the way to that road."

"Six miles short." I said mostly to myself as I peered out the window at the endless wilderness below.

"You're lucky those people with the sat phone came across you, you wouldn't have lasted much longer out there in your condition," said Brad.

We flew north over the mountains for 25 minutes. "Where are we going?" I asked.

"South Lake Tahoe, Barton Memorial hospital."

"Sounds good to me, that's where I was trying to hike to anyway..."

"They'll fix ya up." said George. "You're going to want to remember this view coming up here, it's one of the most spectacular views in the world."

Before long, the giant lake, surrounded by high pine forest covered mountains came into view. The sun was dwindling on the smoky western horizon and the hazy blood red twilight lit the water as if it were on fire. I glanced over at George who had his hands behind his head, taking it all in with a smile. "No hands! These birds fly themselves these days..."

We floated towards the setting sun, towards the great blue lake. Brad continued monitoring my vitals, communicating with the hospital, updating them on my condition. I tried not to listen to the details but I did catch the phrase 'hot load' again. Then he said it was time for another shot. I extended my arm for him and he expertly found a vein and pumped in more of the sweet nectar. An hour ago I was laying in a sun-scorched canyon being circled by vultures, waiting to die. Now I was flying into the Tahoe alpenglow, high on top grade drugs. *Lucky.* Soon we were flying over the southern shore of the lake. We circled out over the deep blue water, then back towards shore. We began descending. I noticed the circles of the heli pad with the big H on top of the hospital. A team of doctors and nurses was waiting on the roof.

As soon as we were on the ground, George powered down the heli, the door opened, my stretcher was loaded onto a gurney and rolled towards the rooftop door. As I was rolled down the hallway to the ER, I noticed the shocked faces of people catching a glimpse of me as I was pushed by. That bad eh folks? I thought. I was officially a trail warrior, *part of the club.* The next few hours were a blur as they hooked me up to machines, attached IV's pried, prodded, poked, tested and ultimately determined I had the same affliction that I had suffered from 2 years prior. I had an inflammation of my pericardium and it had been putting pressure onto my heart disrupting it from pumping blood normally. I was also extremely dehydrated and completely emaciated. I had left it all out on the trail. *The trail had won.*

Lake Tahoe

I was in the hospital for 5 days. They consisted of 3 high calorie meals a day. A steady morphine drip. A bed fit for a king. It was glorious. According to Dr. Wilson my heart had 'suffered damage' and would take between 6 months and a year to heal, if I was lucky. *No problem there*. They monitored my condition closely waiting for the inflammation to go down and after 5 days decided I was stable enough to let me back out into the streets.

"You need to take it easy, it's going to be months before you're fully recovered."

"Does that mean my hike is finished?"

"YES, your hike is finished. If you go back out there you *will* die."

"What about hitchhiking?"

Wilson gave me a strange look and laughed, thinking I was kidding. I wasn't. During the past five days, in my opiate haze, I had decided I would transfer from the *Pacific Crest Trail* to the *Pacific Coast Highway.* Hitchhike to Seattle. I had some friends up there. *Fuck it.*

As I was checking out at the front desk, I asked if there was a campground near the hospital. "Across the street." the receptionist said hesitantly as she looked at me like I couldn't be serious. Apparently transferring from the ICU to tent camping wasn't 'recommended.'

Dusk settled in. I hobbled across the street into the campground. Under the weight of my pack I could hardly walk. I was an 80 year old man again. Kids ran around like crazed bandits through the dark. Massive motor homes, RV's, campers and a few intermittent tents lined the narrow campground roads. Wall to wall. Fires crackled, marshmallows lit ablaze, drunken laughter echoed. It was very dark. I was *high as fuck* on morphine, completely disoriented. I hobbled toward the camp office. It was closed for the night. I hobbled around for 20 minutes, then collapsed in an open patch of ground to pitch the Kelty. I was able to get my tent set up. I crawled in, smoked a bowl, smoked another bowl, then one more.

I woke in the morning to the sounds of the campground coming to life from the cold night. Babies crying, kids running and laughing, dogs barking, birds chirping their morning tunes.

I smoked 5 bowls upon waking up and climbed from my tent in a cloud of smoke. I walked over to the campground office to check in and pay for my spot.

"That'll be 64 dollars." said a mean looking monster of a woman behind the till. I noticed her name tag said Debbie.

"I've just got a small tent, not an RV,"

"That *isssss* the tent price sir," she snapped. "RV's are 85 a night."

"64 to pitch a tent on a 10 by 10 patch of ground eh Deb? How do you *sleeeep* at night?"

"I sleep just *fiiiiiiiine!*" She chirped back in a thick southern drawl.

I gave her the cash and told her I would be checking out immediately. I found the showers, lingering under the hot water for thirty minutes. I packed my tent, headed for the laundromat that was connected to the camp office. I put in a load and sat in the waiting area studying the South Lake Tahoe map I had picked up in the lobby, trying to figure out my next move. My laundry finished, I packed up and walked gingerly out of the campground, across the road to a coffee shop. I ordered a coffee, found a table to think. I overheard a man talking at the table next to mine that sounded like a local.

"You wouldn't happen to know of any campgrounds around that aren't 65$ a night would you?"

"There's a free backpackers campground up on Luther Pass, out of town."

"How far out?"

"7 miles."

I finished my coffee, then walked across the parking lot to an authentic looking taco joint. I ate three tacos, then stopped at a grocery store, loaded up on non-perishables. Cliff bars, soup, cookies. The essentials. I hobbled out to the main road and held out my thumb. It was late afternoon. Before long a beat up 4 runner pulled over. I walked over, it was a chill looking kid about my age with long brown hair.

"Where you headed?"

"Luther pass campground."

"I'm not going that far but I can get you up to the junction on the edge of town that goes up there." I hopped in. His name was Martini.

We slogged through the slow traffic, then he dropped me off on the corner at the edge of town.

I stood on the side of the road once again with my thumb out. Twenty minutes passed, a large rusty old pickup truck pulled over. This guy looked like a carpenter. He sounded friendly enough.

"I'm going past Luther, hop in."

I hopped in. His name was Roy, he was a local contractor. He asked about the hospital bracelets around my wrist. I hadn't been able to get them off yet.

"They rescued me 50 miles south of here."

"How far you hiking?"

"Apparently I'm done hiking, doc said my heart is toast. I'm going to try to hitch-hike up to Seattle."

He looked at me like I was crazy. I was. For some strange reason, the heli rescue had made me feel invincible. A complete lack of fear. It felt very good. Soon, he pulled over.

"Ok this is it, back in those trees. Best of luck out there on the road."

"Thanks, I'm going to need it."

I hopped out, there was nothing but a narrow path back into the woods. It was getting dark. I walked into the forest. Soon I came upon the backpackers campground. It was mostly empty, a few small tents set up intermittently in the makeshift spots. We were up in the mountains in the high pine forest away from everything. It was quiet. A small stream gurgled around the outside of the camp. I walked all the way to the back and set up the Kelty in an open spot on the far edge of camp. Even the small amount of exertion it took for me to walk through camp and set up my tent caused my heart to pound. It was 2,000 ft up above town at nearly 9,000 feet. It wasn't ideal but it was a lot better than Debbie's 3 ring circus. It was *free*. For the next two days I didn't leave camp. I huffed down bowls, pills, cliff bars and cookies. Stayed in a deep haze. Laying in my tent, reading, sitting by the gently flowing stream listening to Jazz and contemplating my next move. Laying in my tent the second night, listening to the crickets and gurgling stream, I decided to hitchhike into town the following day and head to the public library to see what the *craigslist ride share* situation looked like.

I had used *craigslist* to catch rides out of Bozeman a few times. It was always interesting and sometimes even got you to your desired destination. After much drug-saturated thought my plan was to try to head north towards Oregon on the i-5, stop by Eugene, then go west towards the coast, hitchhike up the 101 along the ocean. Foolproof.

I emerged from the haze and started my journey towards town around ten the next morning, walking slowly down the highway with my thumb out. I made it a couple miles before a nice older lady picked me up who was going into town to work at a flower shop. She dropped me off when we rolled into town and I hopped on the city bus heading east down the shore towards the library. The public library was across the street from the lake tucked back in amongst tall Jeffrey pines. I walked in, found a computer, pulled up *craigslist rideshare* rides offered for all of California. The pickings were slim. The only option heading to Oregon for the entire week simply said, *"oakland to portland leaving 8pm. wednesday. doug."* The red-eye from Oakland to Portland blazing up the i-5 through the night. What could possibly go wrong? I sent him a message. "Still got room for a passenger to Eugene?"

Now, normally when I've used *craigslist rideshare* in the past there have been multiple options and through trial and error, I've found the best strategy is to send out several inquiries, flush out the one most likely *not* to rape, kill or fashion a necklace out of your fingers & toes. It's like uber without *any* of the security measures. It also has a reputation of being where the underbelly of society tends to conduct a majority of their business. I once turned down a ride from a guy who wanted to drive 400 miles out of his way and was willing to push back his planned date of departure 10 days to pick me up in as he described it a 'van full of tools'. Had I not called to 'vet' him I'd probably be mounted on his wall or *frozen solid* in his freezer.

Most of the ride-givers where people down to their last dollar driving around desperately picking up anyone they could to keep gas in the tank. They were all characters. Usually it was clear after talking to the person for a minute or two the general level of sketchiness that would be involved. Sometimes it was a bit harder to tell what was rolling towards you until they showed up. I didn't bother calling Doug...didn't want to know.

I walked out of the library, down the shore towards Heavenly ski resort on the state line. It was yet another extremely hot bluebird summer day. Sailboats coasted slowly in the hot breeze. Water-skiers launched walls of spray into the blue sky. Sunbathers, swimmers, walkers, combers, joggers, dogs, littered the white sandy beach. Fisherman casting lines off the pier. College aged kids filled the decks of the beachfront bar-grill drinking, dancing. Further down the shore I walked past the yacht club where sophisticated looking locals sipped their 67' Chateau Margaux and admired their freshly waxed schooners bobbing along the docks. I decided to get *high as a Georgia pine* and head to the Heavenly movie theater to get out of the sun and heat for the afternoon. The theater was located in the Heavenly resort square just past where the gondola launched towards the summit. I sat on the edge of the fountain, smoked a joint, popped a few pills, then walked into the glorious air conditioned theater. I bought a ticket, filled up a glass full of ice-water, bought some Junior Mints and found a seat in the nearly empty theater. About ¾ of the way through the movie my phone lit up with a new message. I flipped it open.

"there room"

"Count me in Doug" I quickly sent back before I could think about it too much. It was Monday afternoon. I had two days to get to the i-5 where Doug would be passing through.

After the movie, I walked slowly back along the shore of Lake Tahoe, taking in the beautiful scene of the late-July evening. The beach had quieted down, the lake sparkled in the soft light, the mountains behind me turned red-gold in the last slanting rays before dusk. I walked across salmon colored sand, along the shoreline. When the public beach turned to private residences I walked up into the neighborhood through the sleepy streets. The houses were vintage 60's style, updated and meticulously cared for. After several blocks, the street I was on connected back to the main road and I started looking for a bus stop. I realized I needed to grab a bite to eat and start my journey back up to Luther Pass if I was going to make it before dark. I hopped off the bus on the west side of town near the local taco joint I had eaten at a few days prior, ordered up 4 soft shells, an ice-water, and ate outside on the patio overlooking the shimmering lake. After dinner, I walked back out to the main road and held out my thumb.

The cars streamed by. Twenty minutes passed until finally a late 80's rusted out red Camry with a plastic tarp for a back window screeched to a stop just past where I was standing. The passenger window rolled down and a cloud of smoke came wafting out. I walked over to the window, peered in through the haze. A man sat in the drivers seat. He had long sun-bleached hair, a tie dye bandanna wrapped around his head, no shirt, no shoes, blue and white swim trunks on. He had an enormous tattoo of an Indian chief on his chest and looked somewhere between late-thirties and mid-forties.

"Hooooop oooonn innnnn! Names Rodney, friends call me Rodahki..."

I eased into the pile of fast food wrappers that covered the front seat.

"Where you headed!?"

"Thanks Rodski, Jack, I'm going up to Luther Pass backpackers campground."

"Cowboy hops! I'll getcha to the road that goes up there!"

As I soon found out, Rodski had woken up on the beach in Tahoe on the morning after his 21st birthday (having started the night in LA) with no recollection of how he got here, and never left. He taught sailing lessons in the summer and ran his own 'retail business' in the winter so he could ski Squaw Valley every day. He passed me the joint he was working on. We started talking skiing and I found out he had skied many a day at Squaw with the late ski legend Shane McConkey.

"McConk was cowboy hops..." he said in a Spanish accent which launched him into an uncontrollable laughing fit that sent him into an uncontrollable coughing fit that lasted several minutes. He was finally able to quell the hacking by popping the lid off his 44 ounce gas station plastic soda cup and frantically guzzling 39 of the 44 ounces of bright green liquid. "Faaaaawwwck yea." he gasped when he finally came up for air.

A few miles down the road the Camry began to shake and jerk as a loud clanking noise began coming from under the hood. Behind us, thick blue-gray smoke billowed out in a steady stream.

"Come on there Betsy!" Rodney said as he gently patted on the dash..." Not tonight girl! We are riding dirtier than a god damn coal miner... Hum on! Hum on! Hum on! Hum on!" he chanted as he gyrated in his seat like he was riding a horse.

"Looks like Betsy's burning oil pretty good" I said.

"Oh she's more than burnin' it..." bellowed Rodski which launched him into another uncontrollable laughing/hacking fit. He desperately poured the remainder of green liquid from the giant plastic cup down his throat like he was putting out a fire. 'Betsy' went silent, we rolled to a stop on the side of the road.

"You fucking hooker Betsy!" yelled Rodney and then started talking to himself. "Ok think Rodski *thiiiink* buddy we don't want to end up back in the slammer bud, let's *hem* shit up *riiiight* this time."

Rodney hopped out, popped the hood and as he lifted it up an enormous cloud of steam and smoke came billowing out.

"Hot Damn!" He slammed the hood back down. Rodney began rummaging around in the back seat, soon emerging with a crowbar. "Got to get these plates off!!" He started prying the front license plate off the car. It looked like he'd been through this routine before. He expertly ripped the screws out of the bumper. Then he rushed to the back of the car, ripped the back license plate off the car, then began prying the trunk open. A steady stream of cars flowed by. Rodski was 'in the zone' (criminally speaking).

Before long he had the trunk open. Out of a pile of empty oil containers he grabbed a large black duffle bag stuffed to the gills. "Okee dookee well Jack sorry but this is as far as this rust bucket goes tonight...Ol' Rodski's gotta *ski-daddle*!" He stuffed the license plates into the duffle bag, then began running barefoot and shirtless through the high grass towards the woods.

And then he was gone, disappearing into the dark pines. Betsy sat sizzling, plastic tarped back window flapping lightly in the breeze of the passing traffic. I started walking down the road, thumb out, hoping for the best, or worst, I didn't want anything in between.

Turns out hitchhiking at night is a very low probability proposition. I walked the remaining 4 miles to the Luther Pass campground under the dim silver light of the moon. A few cars passed by but no one had the balls to pick up a hitchhiker in the dark. I couldn't blame them. The night was cool, almost cold as I made my way into the mountains. The silence of the stars magnified the sounds of the black forest. Its nocturnal inhabitants were up and

moving about snapping twigs, rustling about in the brush.
Walking without my pack wasn't nearly as taxing on my
body but Dr. Wilson wouldn't have approved of the 4 mile
hike. My heart was pounding like a *jackhammer*.

It was well after midnight when I finally walked
into camp. All was quiet. I crawled into my warm sleeping
bag, roasted a bowl, put on some jazz and quickly drifted
off to sleep.

I woke with the sun, began packing up camp. It was
a cold, blue morning, a cool pink glow in the eastern sky. I
brewed coffee, filled the steaming mug as I studied my
map. Estimating travel plans and time frames as a
hitchhiker is damn near impossible, the amount of
unknown variables nearly infinite. It was approximately
100 miles to the i-5 via the Sacramento route,
approximately 250 miles to the i-5 via the Reno to Redding
route which meant anywhere between an hour and a half
and four hours once I was picked up if the vehicle was
capable of going 70 mph and didn't burst into flames. The
amount of time it would take to be picked up could be 5
minutes or 5 hours. At the end of the day I needed to be
somewhere on the i-5 where I would hopefully intersect
Doug and blaze north on the red-eye through the night into
Oregon. I planned to extend my thumb to the universe.
See what would happen. It was all kind of like throwing a
feather into a 45 mph swirling gusty wind and hoping it
ended up in a coffee can 5 miles away.

I-5 (Silk Road of the West)

I finished my coffee, made my way to the highway. In less than five minutes an old crown vic rolled to a stop just past me on the side of the road. At first I thought it was a cop giving me a hard time for hitchhiking, but at second glance it was clear it was a 'former cop car' given a second chance at life (most likely via police auction) by this character. I walked up to the rolled down passenger side window, an old man in with a huge gray beard and even bigger smile looked back at me.

"Where you heading with that monster pack sport?"

"I'm hoping to get to the junction of 50 & 89 7 miles down the road here."

"Hop in!"

Bud looked like Santa Claus. He spent his summers in a small cabin he had built himself in the late 60's just outside Tahoe, in the mountains.

"I remember back in the day I used to ride my thumb all over the west...course back in those days the stories of people being picked up and diced into bite sized pieces were a lot less prevalent."

I glanced over at Bud, he was trying to hold in a smile.

"I'm just fucking with you, you'll most likely be fine out there...no guarantees. Mostly Slicers & Dicers... there may be the odd one in there that'll just tie you up in his rat infested basement and hold you for 20 years..."

Bud guided the Crown Vic back into traffic and yelled "best of luck ol' sport!" as he pulled away.

I crossed the intersection to the corner on the side of the road that was heading out of town on CA 89 to the west up the shore towards Truckee. An hour passed. No ride offers. I've found it's usually quite a bit easier to catch a ride into a town from just outside it or to just outside of town from the edge of it, catching rides out to the open road when it's unclear where you're trying to get to are notoriously much more difficult. (While I wasn't an open-road hitchhiking veteran I had over 2000 successful hitchhikes under my belt up to a small ski resort 16 miles north of Neverland.)

The cars, trucks, campers, and motorcycles streamed by. Another hour passed. No offers. I was baking in the hot mid-day sun and it was nearing noon. I walked into the gas station near the corner, bought an iced tea and a turkey sandwich. I finished the cold tea and sandwich, walked back to the corner. A new pickup truck pulling a massive RV pulled over onto the shoulder of the highway.

I walked up to the rolled down window, a small, pretty blonde woman in her 50's sat in the passenger seat, a big athletic looking man despite his age (early 60's) with a Wisconsin shirt on and a friendly smile leaned over toward the window and asked where I was trying to get to. I explained that I was trying to get to anywhere on the i-5 where I had a ride lined up for later that night.

"We're heading to Redding for Cindy's parent's birthday party we've got plenty of room hop in!" I threw my pack in the back of the truck and hopped in. The man extended his massive hand back toward me.

"I'm Ed, this is my wife Cindy."

"I'm Jack, nice to meet you both. I see your shirt there are you from Wisconsin?"

"Nope, I played football for them in the early 70's. Cindy and I met there during college. We've lived in Southern California for the past 30 years but I just retired, we sold our house and are building one just outside of Reno. Our new house won't be done for another month so we're just traveling around with our RV. We've been camping in South Lake Tahoe for three weeks. What's your story?"

I told them about the trail, leaving out the part about the helicopter rescue and hospital stay. "I'm heading north wherever the road takes me."

"That sounds like one hell of an adventure!"

Ed and I hit it off and we told stories back and forth for the next 3 hours. Ed was an amazing storyteller. He had been a high school principal for 35 years. He had endless stories of the crazy kids that came through during his tenure. We took the 'scenic route' as Ed called it and I couldn't help but notice several signs for the PCT along the way. Most of northern California was on fire and the closer we got to Redding, the thicker the smoke got. As we drove through the thick white cloud, the tall pines 25 feet off the side of the highway were barely visible. Lonely, battered souls slogging north, or south, one step at a time through the thick haze. I thought of Ron, I thought of Mia. Part of me wished I was still out there suffering with them. Most of me was happy I wasn't.

We pulled into Redding, California around 6:00 pm. The thermometer read 101 degrees and the smoke was so thick you couldn't see Mt. Shasta undoubtedly towering to the northeast of town. The smoke illuminated the afternoon light into a bright golden glow. We pulled off the interstate and into a gas station on the edge of the road.

"What time did you say that ride was coming through town?"

"Between 10:30 and 11:30 tonight, the red-eye. I can just waste some time around here, maybe walk down along the river for awhile until Doug comes rolling through."

"Nonsense!" Ed bellowed, "you're more than welcome to come to the barbecue and hang with us until tonight. They've got a pooool!"

"Yeah the whole family would love to meet you Jack...they'll think we're crazy if we tell them we picked up a hitchhiker and brought him all the way here, unless they meet you." added Cindy.

"Well, I can't say no to that."

We pulled out of the gas station and wound through neighborhoods along the river toward what seemed to be the outskirts of town (it was hard to tell with the thick haze) and into a gated community. Gigantic old homes lined the streets on both sides. Before long we pulled onto a long driveway that wound up to a multi-million dollar mansion.

"As you can see Cindy comes from the upper class," said Ed.

He looked back, smiled, winked.

"Edddiieeee..." Cindy said in a scolding tone. "My parents bought this place so long ago things were cheap back in those days."

Ed laughed. "Ok hun, if you say you were poor I believe you." As he winked again towards me.

"We weren't poor, we were comfortable."

"Quite" said Ed quietly as we pulled up to the massive estate.

We walked into the front entry way and onto a huge rug that looked damn near Persian. The foyer had 30 ft

ceilings and two curved staircases on either side wound up
to the second floor. The chandelier hanging from the
ceiling looked like something that had hung in the *titanic*.
We were greeted by two guys with a tray of drinks and
appetizers. The chef and butler. Ed gave me a soft nudge
with his elbow and another wink. Many possible scenarios
had been swirling around in my head as I stood on the side
of the road this morning, this wasn't one of them. We were
informed the rest of the family was out by the pool and
dinner would be ready in 30 minutes. *Lucky.*

As we walked out into the enormous backyard,
meticulously landscaped with large smooth rocks, massive
old-growth pine trees, a tall ornate white fence around the
outside and a pool that included two levels, a waterfall
gently falling from one into the other. About a dozen
family members swam in or lounged around the pool. Two
kids, a girl that looked college age, several adults in their
30's or 40's, and a very old man and woman that sat in
wheelchairs beside the pool. The kids immediately jumped
from the pool and ran full tilt towards Ed and Cindy and
launched into their arms as they yelled
"Grandpa!!!!Grandmaaaa!!!!!" I stood back just outside the
backdoor and fielded confused looks.

"This is our friend Jack that we met in Tahoe!" said
Ed. He then took me around and introduced me to
everyone by the pool. They included Ed and Cindy's son
and daughters, their kids, Cindy's sister, her daughter, a few
family friends and her Mom and Dad. We sat around the
pool and ate dinner. Chicken, lobster, summer salad, cold
pasta salad, fruit salad, corn on the cob, cookies and ice
cream. Laughing, listening to Ed's stories. After dinner I
checked my phone to see if there was any word from Doug.
All I had heard from him at this point was "yep there room"
and that was days ago. I flipped open the flipper, no word
from Doug. It was 8:30, I figured I should let him know I
was in Redding. I pushed send and walked back to the
party. The family had moved in from the pool to the dining

room. I found a spot on the couch and answered questions from everyone about my 'trip'. I tried to give the version that made me seem the least amount crazy, which wasn't easy. I figured with all they'd done for me the least I could do was provide some entertainment.

My phone lit up with a message from the elusive Doug around 9:45.

"fuk up back loadin bed wont b rolin nort till mornin."

Ed had already let me know that if my ride didn't pan out I was more than welcome to stay the night, they had 7 extra bedrooms.

"Well, if I'm translating this message correctly it appears Doug hurt his back loading a bed tonight so he has postponed his departure time until morning."

"Sleeepoovvverrrrr!!!" bellowed Ed excitedly.

I awoke around nine, hopped through the shower connected to my room, and walked down to the dining room where everyone was gathered around a breakfast spread of pancakes, waffles, coffee cake, 5 different kinds of freshly sliced fruit, 3 different kinds of coffee, jelly, jam, honey, orange juice, apple juice, mango juice, whip cream, ice cream, bacon, eggs, and a plate of cheeses that was mind-boggling. The whole family laughed when they saw the look on my face. *Thank you Doug, I thought.* About that time my phone lit up and there was a message from the man himself. "On rode be comin tru reddin 11:30 meet at am pm on i5."

After breakfast it was nearing 11:00. I packed, walked down one of the staircases into the foyer. I gave everyone a hug and thanked them. Ed, Cindy, and I walked out to the truck, loaded up and set off to find the gas station. On the way Ed pulled over to show me the famous bridge with a clear bottom across the Sacramento river. We walked out on the bridge, lingering in the late morning haze.

We pulled into the gas station around 11:30. As I scanned the parking spots, not knowing exactly what I was looking for, there didn't appear to be anyone waiting for a passenger at first glance. I hopped out, unloaded my pack, then hugged and thanked Ed and Cindy.

I waved as they pulled out. It was good to know there were still people like them out there.

I sat on the hot pavement near the ice-cooler, waiting for Doug. I had no idea what Doug looked like, no idea what he was driving. I did know Doug was, at this point, nearly 11 hours late because he had hurt his back 'loading a bed'. I was *baking* in the California sun. Peak season wildfire smoke so thick I could barely see the pumps.

Out of the haze rolled a late 70's, once upon a time white, rusted out cargo van with no doors, no bumpers, no muffler, mirrors that had been duck taped back on and spare tires on all four wheels. It came flying into the station on two wheels, screeching to a stop across three parking spots. As it flew by the front doors where I was standing I could faintly see the outline of a trailer dragging behind it but it was hard to tell what was on it with all the smoke from the van. When the smoke finally cleared, I could see there was only one item on that trailer. A torn, tattered, piss-stained bed. I picked up my backpack, started hesitantly making my way towards the van. As I approached the driver's side, a 300+ pound man well into his 70's, wearing an oil stained, *severely* battered Stetson, a tattered, stretched out t-shirt and a pair of shorts likely from last century, who looked like life had been beating the *ancient fuck* out of him for most of those years already had the hood popped and was dumping in oil, sloshing, spilling all over the sizzling engine...

"Doug?"

He looked at me, very confused, then after several seconds he mumbled "a ya, I'm Doug, hop in." I couldn't tell if he couldn't remember who I was... or who *he* was. I walked to the other side of the van and as I did the side door slid open and out of a pile of cardboard two California surfer looking guys in their 20's hopped out. "Whooa duuude! are you coming along for the riiiiide?!" A wave of relief rolled over me. Their names were Chad and 'B' and they looked as happy to see me as I was to see them. They explained how they were students down in LA and were on one last adventure for the summer heading up to Portland to visit friends.

They had arrived to meet Doug at 8 o clock the previous night as was originally planned and then Doug said he had postponed the trip until morning because the "damn bed fucked his back."

They looked at Doug, confused, and said, "It's almost dark and we're in the heart of Oakland what are we supposed to do now Doug!?"

"I spose you can sleep in the van" he mumbled. After considering their limited options they had decided that seemed like their best chance at surviving the night and figured Doug would be staying at his place. And then Doug had leaned his seat back and said, "night boys." At this point B looks at me wide-eyed and says, "so we slept in the van...WITH DOUG!"

"Wow. So what's your read on Doug is he dangerous?"

Chad glanced over at B and then replied hesitantly "Doug doesn't say much...but last night, at one point, he leaned back his seat and asked 'you boys want some caaaaaandy?' Our hearts nearly stopped as his hand reached for the side panel in the door and then he pulled out a handful of *Mike and Ikes* he had stuffed in there, held it out to us."

Doug is finally finished pouring I don't know how many quarts of oil into the van. We climbed aboard the steaming rig. Chad and B in the back, me up front with Doug. The inside of the van is a tangle of clutter. The back is packed to the ceiling with nothing but cardboard, and the front is a heap of items you would find in your kitchen and your garage, piled in a jumble of trash. Doug tells me to "just wipe all that shit off the front seat onto the floor." When I finally get squeezed into the rubble it feels like I'm sitting in a dumpster. Doug turns the key, the van rumbles to life pumping enough smoke out of the tail-pipe to turn the heads of everyone at the gas station who start coughing and putting their shirts over their faces. I'm wondering if the van is on fire with the enormous amount of smoke that is accumulating. Doug doesn't seem concerned in the least, he cranks it into gear, we roll out of the parking lot towards the on-ramp for the I-5. We merge into traffic. The van groans and squeals as Doug coaxes it up to speed. Most of northern California is on fire, the wildfire smoke is so thick you can't see more than a mile in any direction and the blistering heat is suffocating. I just settle back into the warm trash and think, well, at least we're moving in the right direction, I still have all my fingers and toes. We don't make it 5 miles outside Redding and Doug takes the off-ramp to a rest area. We screeched to a stop, Doug pops the hood and hops out to take a look. Thirty seconds or so goes by and then he slams the hood back in place, hops back up in the front seat, and as he cranks it back into gear and we lurch forward he mutters, "had to check that oil cap, don't want to forget that oil cap or it's NOT pretty." I'm glad there's no major issue with the engine, not that you'd know it from all the smoke, squealing, and constant smell of burnt rubber. Doug seems pleased with how his rig is running. We get back out on the road passing by lake Shasta, climbing to near the foot of Mt. Shasta. We continue our slog through the haze winding up the smoky mountain roads, the van fully maxed out at 45 mph. Cars are flying by us on all sides. Doug hasn't said much of anything, Chad and B are passed out cold back in the pile of cardboard. Several hours go by, we finally reach Siskiyou summit, the highest point on the i-5. I notice a sign that it's downhill for the next 7 miles and it

indicates several turnouts for out of control vehicles. As
we roll over the crest and start our descent, I can see the
road out in front of us like a long steep ski slope. It feels
like when you go over the crest at the top of a roller coaster
(except this roller coaster car is 40+ yrs old and its
maintenance schedule likely includes dumping enough oil
in to keep it from seizing up and putting out the engine fires
as fast as possible.) We quickly pick up speed and the
commotion wakes Chad and B up in the back. Soon we're
going 85 mph, the van is creaking, bearings are squealing.
The wind whipping through the windows sounds like we're
a jet taking off on a runway. I check the side mirror, the
trailer looks like a sparkler on the 4th of July. The duck-
taped mirror suddenly rips off the side of the van, flies over
the guard rail and disappears down the steep slope into the
green forest below. I look over at Doug, he's completely
cool, one hand on the wheel leaned back with a small grin
on his face. He doesn't have his feet on the gas or the
brakes and the speedometer is creeping past 90. The van
sounds like it's going to start breaking apart, we're weaving
in and out of traffic, flying by any and every car on the
road. I'm gripping whatever I can to stay upright, which is
mostly trash, and I hear Chad and B rolling around back in
the cardboard trying to stabilize themselves however they
can. "You boy's aren't going to want to be back there if she
starts to break up..." mumbles Doug nonchalantly. This
free-fall goes on for several minutes. Finally, we start
leveling out and our speed drops below 100. Chad and B
looked like they had just seen a ghost. I glanced over at
Doug who looked like a little kid at the fair who wanted go
on the ride again. Doug was a cowboy. In lieu of a horse,
he was riding a 1978 cargo van, sans muffler, around the
west on spare tires.

We continued on through southern Oregon and
from what I could see through the haze it was beautiful
country. Thick pine forest covered medium sized
mountains with valleys and canyons strewn about. The

haze finally started to dissipate as we came upon Grants Pass Oregon, a 100 miles or so south of Eugene. Doug took the second exit off the freeway and pulled into a gas station. I figure we must need some gas as he still hasn't filled any since I've been on this ride, but instead of pulling up to the pumps, Doug screeches to a stop in a parking spot in front of the building, leans his seat back and says, "ya boys, can't keep my eyes open, I need a little cat nap here, we'll get back on the road after a bit."

It's 3 o clock in the afternoon.

Chad, B and I hop out and decide to get tacos across the street. We took our time eating and after 45 minutes decided to head back towards the gas station, check to see if Doug is awake yet, but as we approach the van it's clear that he's still passed out in the front seat, face leaned against the window. All we can do is wait. We find a spot in the grass on the opposite side of the gas station where we have a clear view of Doug so we can keep an eye on him and the van. Another half hour passes.

Suddenly, three squad cars along with two unmarked cars come flying into the station and surround Doug's van on all sides boxing him in. Deputy sheriffs and US marshals hop out, using the cars as cover, guns drawn, all pointed squarely on Doug, who is still sleeping like a baby in the driver's seat. One of the deputies produces a megaphone and yells "You are completely surrounded! Slowly step out of the vehicle with your hands in the air!" Nothing. Doug is still comatose. "Step OUT of your vehicle with your hands in the AIR!" Doug doesn't so much as flinch. "This is your LAST warning! SLOWLY step out of your vehicle with your ARMS in the AIR!" Comatose. The mob of lawmen cautiously shuffled towards the van, billy clubs, guns in hand. As if approaching a caged tiger. (Doug's face is leaned against the driver side window with his nose and lips smashed against the glass.) They rip the door open and Doug is startled back to life as he falls hard to the pavement. He attempts to curl up into a ball. They pounce on him and quickly cuff his hands behind his back. The five of them then struggled for 15 minutes to load all 300+ pounds of Doug into the back of a squad car. Doug wasn't resisting, but he certainly wasn't helping either. He had gone fully limp and they were dealing with *dead weight*. It looked like they were trying to wrestle a beached whale into the squad car. Doug began laughing hysterically at their ridiculous attempts to lift him, ignoring all threats to cooperate. By the time they managed to load him, Doug had tears streaming down his cheeks and was struggling to catch his breath from laughter. After the cops had Doug loaded into the squad car, they drove towards the exit, merged back into traffic. Doug winked at us through wet eyes on the way by.

We hurried over to the van, slid open the side door. Chad and B grabbed their packs out from the pile of cardboard. As they were grabbing the packs a large man dressed in a pair of jeans, a flannel shirt with the sleeves cut off, cowboy boots and hat walked up to the van, opened the driver's door, hopped in and tried to start it. The van didn't make so much as a click.

"Sonofa Bitch!" the man yelled as he violently slammed his hands on the dash. He still hadn't acknowledged us or the fact that we were taking our packs from the van.

"Let's get out of here!" I mouthed to Chad and B and we ran like hell. Well, they ran, I hobbled, heart beating like a *jackhammer*. Once we were completely gassed and a safe distance away from the van and mystery cowboy, we stopped to figure out a plan. After weighing our meager options, we decided to spray-paint *Portland* on a piece of cardboard B had grabbed from Doug's surplus pile. Roll the dice out on the I-5. It was around 5 o clock on a Thursday afternoon, there were thousands of cars roaring by on the four lane freeway. We made our way up the on ramp and onto the side of the road, spread out in a line a few hundred feet apart, Chad up front holding the *Portland* sign. I was behind both of them continually looking behind me to check if anyone had pulled over. A couple hours passed, we're offered a few rides but they're for a small town 30 miles down the road. The mid-summer sun was sinking fast on the horizon and we all agreed if we didn't get a ride in the next 10 minutes we would find a spot to 'cowboy camp' around Grants Pass, try again in the morning. My phone rang, it was Truman.

"How's it going out west?"

"Well, I was rescued by a helicopter from the wilderness, just released from the hospital, I'm hitchhiking north on the i-5. My last ride was arrested mid-ride 20 minutes ago. It's going *decent.*"

"What!?"

I looked behind me and could not believe my eyes. On the side of the freeway was a black Porsche convertible.

"A car just pulled over, I'll call tomorrow!"

I hurried over to it, a gorgeous woman in maybe her mid 30's was sitting in the driver's seat. She had long blond hair, stunning stony blue eye's full of mischief, wore a silky flowing summer dress and had the type of beauty that caused men to stop breathing when she walked into a room.

"Hey there...where are you boy's headed?"

"We're trying to get to Eugene tonight if we can."

"Well that's where I'm going and I'm bored as hell! Hop in boys let's go for a riiide!" Chad and B were already running towards the car and looked elated when I gave them the thumbs up. We loaded our packs into the front trunk, hopped in. She peeled out into traffic like we were shot out of a cannon leaving long black streaks on the side of the road while simultaneously lighting up a joint...and then she says, "you boys are probably going to want to buckle up this thing's got some serious balls and I drive like a fucking sailor on shore leave!"

Her name was Eleanor. She was not kidding. Eleanor was quite the lady, and one hell of a driver. She told us how she had been a ski racer back in the day and had lived and skied all over the west for several years before marrying some rich 'asshole' in Aspen when she was in her late 20's. But the life of a trophy wife never fit her and she had divorced him a few years later. It wasn't all bad, she said, "I got a few mill and a daughter out of the deal."

"105...107...110...115...yahooooooooo! Get out the WAYYYY!" She hollered as we whizzed by cars going the speed limit like they were parked on the side of the road.

I was pinned to the back of the passenger seat enjoying every minute of it. Also thinking our second ride of the day was going to be taken into custody at any moment.

"FREE DOUG!" we chanted as we tore through the blue moon night like a Japanese bullet train off the tracks.

Eleanor drove the 100 miles to Eugene in under an hour, she said we could sleep at her place. We stopped for Chinese on the way to her house and fought over who would get to buy her dinner. Ellie lived in a very nice house not far from the Oregon Ducks campus. She had a fire pit in the backyard along the river. We sat around the fire telling stories well into the night. Chad and B finally went off to bed and it was just the two of us. Ellie came over and sat on my lap in her black yoga pants, said she was cold. I was *hard*. She turned her head towards me, smiled. I kissed her lightly. We kissed next to the fire, then I carried her up to the master bedroom. We kissed furiously all the way. When we made it to the bed we both started ripping each others clothes off. When I got her pants off I dipped a finger inside. She was very wet already. She kissed me with more and more enthusiasm as I continued to play with her. Then I was on my back on the bed and she had me in her mouth, up and down she licked and sucked slowly and lightly at first and then fast and furious, when I couldn't hold on any longer I stopped her so I could cool down. "You have such a nice cock!" she said excitedly. I grabbed the honey bear from my pack, squeezed out a big mound. Then I went to work with my tongue, lapping up the honey. She moaned louder and louder pulling gently on my hair and curling her toes way up in the air. When I had cleaned off all the honey I worked my way up her sexy body, kissing her as I slowly worked my way inside. She bit my lip gently. I started slow and steady and worked into a furious pace as she whispered *harder harder harder harder* in my ear. She looked at me, smiled, then started clenching gently at just the right moment every stroke. I didn't last long after that, and we embraced as I jerked and shook in ecstasy. As we drifted off to sleep I thought about how whether or not I survived this journey I could potentially have children all the way up the West Coast.

The next day I borrowed a bike from the garage, rode down to Oregon State's campus. The Ducks. I pedaled down Pre's trail along the Willamette river looking for people who looked like they had weed. Recreational had been approved by the Oregon voters at the last election but they weren't going to open up the dispensaries to the masses for a few more months. I rode along the path, through the outskirts of campus. Before long, I spotted a kid with a tie die shirt on, hair to mid-back, leather thong sandals and eye's that were cherry red. I approached and asked if I could buy a little weed. He held up a bag with one nug in it.

"Sorry this is aaaalllll I haaavve with me. Go ahead and take this braaaaa."

I thanked him and biked back to Eleanor's. Chad and B were sitting in the driveway waiting for their next *craigslist rideshare*. They were waiting for a guy named Jarvis who was headed up to Portland. They hadn't talked to him on the phone, just answered a *craigslist* add that said he had run out of gas, money, and hope in Eugene and he needed riders to fill the tank to help him continue his push north. Eleanor and I waited with them in the driveway, she kept leaning over to me and whispering how fast she was going to get me off when they left. I had to sit down in a lawn chair just thinking about it.

An hour had gone by when we heard a faint yet deep rumble that seemed to be getting closer. A diesel V.W. van from long ago rounded the corner on two wheels like it was running from the cops. A steady stream of dark black smoke streamed behind it. It puttered and missed several times, then went completely silent when it was a block away. A man had his head out the driver's side window. He wore a brightly colored Hawaiian shirt and an African safari bucket hat. He had thick glasses with frames that were huge on his small skinny, scruffy face. As he coasted up to the house in silence, he pounded on the side of the van with his hand coaxing it into the driveway. The door creaked loudly as he opened it and hopped out. He was shockingly small. Five foot five, maybe 120 pounds with a smile from ear to ear. He looked both friendly and crazy at the same time.

"You folks wouldn't happen to have a gas can with diesel by chance!? Well shiiiit are you Chad and B!?"

"Jarvis?"

"Jarvis Scanlin at your service," he said with a small curtsy. "Ol' trusty rusty here is ready to teleport you boys to Portland just as soon as she gets some gas in the tank."

"Sorry Jarvis, I only have unleaded for the lawnmower, but there's a gas station down a couple blocks, around the corner." said Eleanor.

"We'll walk down there with you Jarvis, said Chad."

"Sounds like a plan boy's, put my last dime in this morning. Completely tapped. Not to worry though, I'm heading up towards Portland with a hot tip on where to find

D.B.'s cash. It's pretty far back in there but I've got a cooler full of fresh roadkill that should hold me over and plenty of darts, I *should* be good to go as long as you guys get me up to Portland." Jarvis said as he lit up the stub of a dart.

As we watched the trail of diesel smoke disappear over the hill, Eleanor and I chuckled at the beautiful sight. We then ran for the house and embarked on a 3 day sex bender. The only time we left the house was to go out to the best restaurants in Eugene and stop off at the market for cheese, chocolate, honey, steaks, and plenty of freshly picked produce from the farmer's market. It was blackberry season. I had never been fucked so good in my life. Up and down, around and around we went. One blur of pleasure.

Despite temptation to stay in this mystical woman's arms forever, I was ready to hit the coast and head north along the ocean. As I studied my maps, trying to figure out how to hitchhike out of Eugene, Eleanor sat down beside me on the couch and cuddled in my arms. "Let's go out to the beach tomorrow, we can spend the day together and then I'll drop you off wherever you want. I still think you should just stay here for awhile, but I understand," she said as she gave me a look that could have tamed lions.

The magnificent Pacific rolled, a dark blue against the pearl gray sky. High cliffs of lava rocks cradled the booming surf. Ellie rode me like a bull back in a secluded cove as the cold salty water inched closer and closer to us with every wave. We made our way back up the path through the damp seaside forest as the cool evening breeze began to blow off the water.

We ate dinner in Florence at a locally owned seafood joint along the docks. The late evening sun lingered where the dark blue water met the golden red dusk.

After dinner I had Eleanor drop me off in the sand dunes south of town. The ocean rolled in on the dunes.

"You are crazy." she said with a smile.

"I'm very happy I met you Eleanor, thanks for the ride."

I kissed her one last time, picked up my battered pack from the trunk of the Porsch, then stumbled into the dunes.

Pacific Coast Highway

-The Great Hitchhike North-

I was back on my own. Back in the wild. *The great hitchhike north.* I walked way back into the dunes and found a place to set up camp among a patch of trees. I could hear the ocean, but couldn't quite see it through the dunes and foliage. The next morning I walked 1.5 miles into downtown Florence, the place (arguably) best known for, back in the summer of '79, stuffing a giant whale that had washed up on the beach full to the gills with dynamite and lighting the fuse. Pieces of rancid rotting whale flesh had rained down on Florence for nearly 10 minutes covering a good portion of town. One large-ish chunk had totaled a parked car 5 miles away.

The sleepy downtown was quiet. I found a diner to eat breakfast. Three beef and cheese enchiladas and a coffee later I walked north along main street looking for a medical cannabis dispensary. My stash was nearly gone. Before long, I found one tucked back behind an old antique's thrift store. I found a place on a bench near, but not too close to the front door of the dispensary. The place was quiet. Finally, an older guy drove by, pulled a u-turn and parked in front of the bench I was sitting on. He hopped out of the truck and walked towards the front doors before I could catch his attention. On his way out I hopped up and nonchalantly walked towards him trying to look as friendly and non-threatening as possible. I held out a 20 and asked if he could spare a few nugs...his face lit up in a big smile, he reached into the bag, pulled out two huge nugs and put them in my outstretched hand. "Enjoy." I thanked him, walked back towards the dunes with my treasure. I went for a long walk down to the beach, along the shoreline to the south. The rhythmic crashing of the waves was soothing. A strong cool breeze gusted, the navy blue waves rose and fell against the dark gray of the clouds. Sea gulls squawked and dove and walked through the sand straight legged and frantic. The day slipped away like a puff of wind. The burnt orange sun slipped lazily into the Pacific.

The next day I walked up and down the beach, puffing the day away. The white surf boomed. It was another dark, cool, misty day which felt amazing in contrast to the relentless smoke and sun in California. Shorebirds floated on tufts of wind, I floated right along with them. I decided to walk downtown in the morning, eat some enchiladas, drink some coffee, then start walking north along the 101 with my thumb out. See what would happen.

Before long an old shitty white rust-bucket of a hatchback pulled over just down the road from where I was standing. I walked to the passenger side door, opened it, peered in. In the driver's seat sat a frayed looking man in his 50's. He was short, had a huge potbelly and wore old cargo shorts, long socks with a blue stripe across the top pulled up almost to knee length. He wore an old golf shirt that looked like it had been through the wash millions of times. His hair and face looked like he had been struck by lightning. He seemed nervous, which was never a good sign.

"I'm not going north but I live down the road here you wanna go drink a few brewskis?"

"I'm not much of a drinker, got any weed?" I was down to my last nug again and I was desperate to find some more. *Clearly.*

"I can call the weed-lady."

I hopped in the front seat, we squealed off down the road. He soon took a left and we drove down a winding road towards the coast, a mile or two down the road he pulled into a driveway, up to a log A-frame. On the way he talked a mile a minute, constant blabber. Some of it seemed highly intelligent, some sounded like 4th grade gossip. It was constant. I started to wonder if he had lost his mind. Before long that was not a question. His name was Rick. We got out of the car and I could see the ocean sparkling and rolling in the warm morning, hear it crashing into the shore below the cliffs. We walked into the A-frame. Rick continued talking. The kitchen sink overflowed with dishes. A small, very old tv sat back in the far corner. It was playing what looked like an old Olympics gymnastics broadcast from the 80's. Several cats darted around in and out of the random furniture and junk that was strewn all about the room. An old blue ragged sofa sat opposite the tv. A small end table beside it was covered in pill bottles. Between twenty five and thirty bottles. Rick was walking and talking towards the couch. He sat on the far end near the pill bottles. "These here are for my cats."

"You must have some pretty sick cats Rick."

"Well sometimes my cats do share their meds with me."

"Is that so? Do they help?" Rick sat there with a blank stare on his face. Eyes fixed into space. "Still there Rick?" his face snapped back to life.

"Heeelll yea they work. Life changing. Here?" Rick said as he filled his palm with pills and extended them towards me.

"I don't doubt they're life changing, I'll pass."

"Suit yourself." Rick said as he tossed the palm full of pills into his mouth.

"How about that weed? You said you had to make a call."

"Yeesss." Rick pulled a flip phone out of his pocket, selected a number and pressed send. There was no answer. Rick dialed again. No answer. Rick dialed again. No answer. Rick dialed again. Rick dialed again. This went on for almost a minute before I suggested he maybe give it a few, give them a chance to see the 19 missed calls.

"Wiiiiiiillllll do"

We sat there and waited. Rick realized gymnastics was on the television and hurried towards the tv, then quickly switched it off in what seemed like embarrassment. I noticed 40-50 VHS tapes piled in a high stack alongside the tv, all with Olympic rings hand drawn along with a year written in bold, all caps. Rick launched into a 10 minute ad lib monologue on why there had been gymnastics playing on the tv. For some reason he was terribly embarrassed by the gymnastics. His rambling monologue varied from vehemently denying that he was a fan of gymnastics at all, that the tapes weren't his and neither was the tv for that matter, to explaining why he was a fan of gymnastics along with incredible amounts of facts on stats about various gymnasts from the mid 60's on. At some point, the handful of pills seemed to take effect and Rick started slurring terribly. The amount of shit he reeled off about gymnastics was incredible. He closed his monologue with a complete denial that he even knew what the sport was.

I was starting to get a bad feeling about the whole situation. I realized that this was how those stories start out that end with - 'and then he locked the poor bastard in the basement for 20 years'. The red flags were popping up like gophers on the Montana prairie. Some of them I could write off as maybe nothing, but the fact that Rick was tee'd up on his cat's pills certainly wasn't helping his case. His frayed, nervous, *blasted* demeanor was putting me on edge and finally I couldn't sit there anymore. I got up, threw my pack over my shoulders and headed for the door.

"Well nice to meet you Rick I better be going, gotta get back on that road." Rick quickly popped off the couch and followed.

"What about the weeeeed, man!?" Rick said desperately.

I slipped my boots on, quickly turned the knob and got out of the house. When I was halfway down the driveway I looked back towards the cabin, Rick was standing in the doorway. *A crazed madman.* I walked as fast as I could to get down the road where there were other houses. I made it down the road a half mile or so when I heard the roar of an engine coming down the road. I whirled around, it was Rick's hatchback heading straight at me.

I made for the ditch, Rick whizzed past me, then whirled into a violent u-turn 20 feet down the road. He screeched to a stop alongside me. Head hanging out the window like a dog, holding his phone up in the air like a trophy, he says... "Got a hold of the weed laaaady!!!!"

"Thanks Rick but I really need to be moving on here."

"But I gotta hoooooold of her maaaaan we could smoookke some weeeed!!!!" Looking more insane, electrified than ever.

"More for you bud, I've really got to be going." I said as I walked back up onto the road behind Rick's car and continued walking. Rick's car sat there stationary.

Sitting. Then I heard his engine revving violently over and over. I looked back, getting ready to make for the ditch. Rick let the clutch out and squealed his tires for 25 feet down the road in the opposite direction, fish-tailing back and forth several times. The final fishtail he almost drifted fully horizontal to the road, towards the woods, but managed to stay on the blacktop and disappear in a cloud of burnt rubber.

Before long I was back out on the 101 with my thumb out. I made it a half mile north of town before an old pickup with a camper on the bed pulled over. I walked up to the passenger side window. A Scandinavian looking guy with blond hair, blue eyes and bright yellow board shorts smiled back.

"Where ya headed?"

"North."

"Hop in!"

Ole was Swedish. He had quit his high paying job in Stockholm a year ago, headed first to Japan for a few months, catching prime pow season. When the snow stopped falling there he headed to Chile and spent 5 months skiing the Chilean steeps. When the snow stopped falling there, he started his journey north surfing the entire west coast of South America and the US all the way to British Columbia where he planned to spend the following winter skiing Rogers Pass.

We stopped at a surf shop in Rockport and Ole bought a new surfboard. I used his old one and for the next 4 days we camped and surfed along the coastline just north of Rockport. I hadn't done much surfing and wasn't any good but it felt great to be in the cold salty water and get worn out by the power of the waves. I managed to catch a few every day and quickly understood the addictive quality surfing is notorious for. Each night we bought fresh vegetables, potatoes along with a cut of meat and cooked up hobo style dinners on the campfire. Ole told stories of his travels and I told stories from mine. On the fifth morning we rolled into Lincoln Beach, stopped at the public library. Ole wanted to research surf spots and tide reports. I wanted to see what lay to the north, camping spots along the way.

Ole decided to go back south and hit a notorious wave down by Florence that he had missed. I decided to hold out my thumb, launch the torpedo north. Ole dropped me on the side of the road just north of Lincoln Beach.

I began walking down the narrow shoulder with my thumb out. It was mid-morning, the 101 was very busy. Cars zoomed by in both directions. After walking for 20 minutes down the narrow shoulder, I heard the roar of an engine accelerating aggressively. I spun around and an old blue mustang convertible was flying head on towards oncoming traffic in the seaside lane. I darted off into the woods just as he found another gear and swerved right at me, narrowly missing the oncoming traffic as he fishtailed back and forth, tires desperately trying to grip the road and avoid the woods on the right, 100 ft. cliffs down to the sea on the left, and steady oncoming traffic who screeched and swerved in panic. The traffic tornado moved on down the road past me. Twenty seconds later 4 sheriffs cars came blaring and roaring right on by. *Doug?*

I made it past the junction that headed towards Salem and the I-5. Most of the cars seemed to be going inland. I continued down the road for 5 minutes, then held my thumb out. I waited with no luck for more than an hour. Another hour went by. Not many cars went by. The white sun beat down relentlessly, my water dwindled. I was being cooked alive on the side of the highway. Just as I was about to give up until evening and walk back towards town, a damn near brand new bmw convertible with the top up pulled over. I walked up to passenger side door and a beautiful woman in maybe her late 30's looked back at me with a wry smile. Before you get in, take off your shirt and shorts so I know you aren't armed. You can leave your boxers on, for now. I looked back at her waiting for the cue that she was kidding and then realized she wasn't kidding. I took off my shirt and shorts threw them in the back seat with my pack, then hopped in. We sped North along the coast. Amy was going to Astoria to visit her brother and his family who owned a salmon fishing boat and was ashore for a few days. In three hours we were pulling into Astoria, Oregon.

I stopped to eat at a burger joint below the 4 mile bridge across the Columbia River. As I was ordering I asked the girl at the till if it was ok to walk across the bridge.

"I've seen someone do it once."

"How long have you lived here?"

"My whole life."

I ate my hamburger slowly, overlooking the bay sparkling in the quiet evening sunlight, salmon boats bobbing on the gentle waves. According to the research I had done at the library that morning, there was no camping in Astoria, but just across the bridge in Long Beach Washington there were several camping spots right on the water. I hiked on. *Fuck it.*

As I walked along the narrow shoulder curling around over the water, I passed 4 signs that read *'no pedestrians'.* Traffic whizzed by relentlessly on my left. I made it halfway across the bridge with relatively no incident, then noticed the right lane was closed ahead and there were construction workers holding stop signs directing both lanes of traffic through the left lane. The right lane traffic was currently stopped so I crossed to the other side. I started walking and then noticed a construction pickup truck with a light on top flashing as it drove top speed in my direction. It screeched to a stop near me, a man with a construction hat and red ears jumped out of the driver's side and marched towards me with a furious look on his face as he yelled "NO PEDESTRIANS ON THE BRIDGE! THERE'S A HUGE FINE FOR WALKING ACROSS THIS BRIDGE!"

"I'm 2 miles across, 2 miles to go, I'm going to keep going."

The man's face was cherry red, he looked like he was going to pop with rage.

"Hey! hop in with us we've got room!"

I whirled around, there was a dark blue bimmer sitting first in line, waiting in the right lane of stopped traffic. I loaded into the back and soon it was our turn to pass around the construction. I gave the peace sign to the red eared man on the way past him. He was sucking on a dart with all his might.

A man and woman in their late 40's, Mary and Dave, sat in the front and I was in the back with their 10 year old son Rob.

"We saw that construction guy giving you a hard time."

"Thanks, you really got me out of a jam back there, that guy looked like he was about to have an aneurysm."

"Where are you headed?"

"Long Beach."

"We're going right past there. It's the kite festival right now, biggest event of the year."

Mary and Dave dropped me off in the quaint downtown of Long Beach. The place was crawling with kite fliers. I walked into the first business I passed, a costume shop. There was an elephant standing at the till, I asked the elephant where the nearest weed dispensary was in town. I could almost feel the first hit...

"None in town yet...nearest one would be an hour inland, Longview, I would guess."

I felt like I had been punched in the gut. I was a junkie.

It was already dusk, I needed to find a place to camp. I stopped at a general store on the edge of town, asked where the nearest campground was.

"One mile down the road but that thing is surely booked to the gills this weekend with the kite festival, you'd be wasting your time to walk down there. A half mile south on the right there is a trail out to the beach, but you'll have to be careful to stay out of sight, there's a fine for camping on the beach and they'll be sure to be out this weekend with the festival."

I found a narrow path through the trees and walked toward the sound of the ocean. Before long I popped out on the beach and into the dim light of the blush colored twilight sky. The dark water foamed and rolled below. A chilly breeze hit me off the water, I needed to get camp set up before dark. I walked a few hundred yards down the beach through the cool, soft sand, ducked back in the trees and found some pine bushes with an open area between them. It was just big enough for a small tent and the pine trees would provide cover. I got the battered Kelty set up between the pines and walked toward the soothing sound of the waves. I stood there in the burgundy dusk, on the shores of the mighty Pacific. Against all sensible odds I was still in one piece after another wild day on the road. My ridiculously good luck seemed to be holding.

I woke to the crashing of waves, light was just coming low in the east, breaking along the grey ridges, and a cold rim of moon still hung over the ocean. It was very cold. I crawled out of the tent, quickly packed up camp, and walked with my pack out of the trees onto the white sandy beach. A thick fog hung over the water. The cold damp air was refreshing. Like taking a cold shower in the morning. I could see the faint outline of a fishing boat bobbing up and down way out in the waves. I walked down the beach for a mile to warm up, then back toward the path to town. I walked into town just as the hazy August sun was peeking up over the horizon, found a local diner that was open. I noticed several kites tangled in the overhead power lines. I walked in and ordered toast, bacon, eggs and coffee After breakfast I walked south towards the junction on the edge of town with highway 4 that headed east. I held out my thumb. Soon a ford focus pulled over and a man that looked like a used car salesman who hadn't sold a car in a *long* time rolled down the window, "where are ya headed?"

"Longview."

"I'm not going that far east, but I can get you down the road a ways."

Roger was a traveling salesman who had lived in Washington his whole life. He was 55. We chatted about the tides for a half hour, then reached a junction where you had the option to continue east or head north. "Sorry but I've got to head north for a meeting." Roger said as he pulled over.

"Thanks for the ride Rodge."

"No problem, best of luck."

I found a spot, held out my thumb. I stood there for an hour. Three cars passed. It was quiet except for the chatter of bugs and birds. There is something eerie about a quiet highway. Like there is a reason no one is there. I waited. A few more cars passed but none of them where up to roll the dice on a hitchhiker. Another half hour went by. A very old suburban approached from the east on highway 4. It slowed as it approached the junction and then 50 yards before it reached me it slowed to a stop on the shoulder of the opposite side of the highway. It was at least 20 years old and had been given a home-made camo paint job. Its engine rumbled in a low growl as it occasionally missed and gurgled and hiccupped, almost died but somehow pulled through each time just when it sounded like it would surely quit. A man in a camo jacket sat in the front seat. The suburban sat there rumbling. The highway was quiet in both directions. The beast of a vehicle sat there rumbling. The driver was watching me. I began to feel more and more uneasy. I began to imagine camo man deciding which body part of mine he was going to cut off first. Deciding how he was going to snare dinner. I felt like helpless prey, decided my best option would be to run for the swamp down the slope behind me, maybe I could lose him in the bog. He sat there rumbling, watching for 10 minutes. Just as his door was beginning to open, I heard loud Cuban music approaching from the west. An ancient Ford Mercury came flying around the curve, screeching to a stop on the side of the road just past where I was standing. All four windows were rolled down, the music echoed in all directions of the quiet highway. I hurried over, opened the driver's side door, hopped in. The driver was a small old man with a big white beard and a wool stocking cap on, suspenders over his checkered flannel shirt and poop colored corduroy pants with burly lumberjack boots on his feet. Monty was on the phone when I got in.

"Hold on woman! I just picked up a hitchhiker... A hitchhiiiikker! Well, he doesn't look like a killer Janny.... I'll call you back you're breaking uuup!" Monty made a crackling noise with his mouth and then flipped the phone closed.

"God damn woman is bat shit crazy no two ways about it!"

"The wife?"

"Girlfriend, I think I'm going to have to cut'er loose here I won't live to see Christmas at this rate."

We rumbled down the winding road in the ancient gray dented Mercury. Monte's phone rang again. "What the hell is it NOW!? HELL YES I'm still alive. Settle. SETTLE DOWN now JANNY! Well he looks like a normal kid with a backpack. Cause he needed a god damn RIDE that's why I PICKED HIM UP! I'm going now." Monty hung up.

We blazed east winding through the thick forest of the Columbia River gorge towards Longview. Bernie continued to answer calls from Janny intermittently. Between calls he told stories from his days as a logger and fisherman. He was a jolly fellow that radiated joy and little did he know it he had probably saved me from my fate at the hands of the *suburban roadside killer*.

We rolled into Longview around 1:00 pm and Bernie pulled into a gas station on the edge of town. I noticed a lake with a walking path around it a quarter mile down the road and decided this would be a good spot to start my search. As Bernie went in to pay, I put an envelope with a stack of hundreds along with a small shred of paper from the top of the envelope that said *"thank you Monty"* in his middle consul. I had found the cash buried deep in my backpack a few days earlier...remnants from the *lower eastside mugger*. Little did that *poor bastard* know how far his charity had reached. Monty came bopping out of the gas station with a huge plastic cup of soda and a bag of popcorn. "Free popcorn with a fill!" he exclaimed, grinning from ear to ear, almost dancing. I just hoped he didn't have a stroke when he found the cash.

I bought a turkey sandwich and an iced tea from the gas station and set off down the shoulder of the road towards the sparkling pond. Before I made it to the pond, I noticed a group of businesses tucked back in the trees. I wandered down the tar road in hopes of finding some green gold. Sure enough one of the storefronts was a dispensary. I walked into it, hands shaking in excitement like a junkie about to tap a vein, and bought a half ounce of several different kinds including a large nug that sat on a small platform in the glass case like a trophy. It had apparently won numerous awards at the Cannabis Cup and according to the kid working had enough THC in it to get an elephant high. He carefully packaged my treasure in small airtight bags. I walked back out into the heat of the day, decided to get baked by the pond.

I found a quiet alcove on the far side, just off the path, then sat on a bench near the green water. I dug my music out of the top pocket of my pack, selected a jazz playlist, then began *the great bake*. Roasting bowls into the afternoon. After my 10th or 11th bowl I passed out on the bench, head resting on my sleeping bag roll. When I came to it was early evening. I had that fresh feeling of complete rest that an afternoon nap will give you. I rolled a large joint, slowly puffed it down as I contemplated what to do next.

I decided to head towards the public library, check the *craigslist ride-share* 'situation'. *Fuck it.* As I made my way across the green lawn of the park I noticed an old woman reading a book in the shade of two old coastal redwoods. "Hi there ma'am, you wouldn't happen to know where the public library is would you?" She looked up at me squinting through the evening sunlight.

"Hop on Olympia Way it will lead you right to it," she said with a kind smile as she pointed behind her to the northeast.

The walk to the library took 30-40 minutes. I noticed how much lighter my pack was starting to feel, my body finally adjusting to the bone crushing weight.

The library was an old historic building. I walked in and was hit by a glorious wave of air conditioning. I walked over to the lady at the front desk. She was a small woman with big glasses and wore a flower-colored summer dress. She looked like she was born to be a librarian.

"Can I get a guest pass for a computer please?" Her face lit up in a full smile as she extended her hand which held a small slip of paper with a code on it.

I walked across the quiet library, found a cluster of computers. The place was empty, it must be a weekday, I thought. I pulled up *craigslist rideshare*. The prospects were slim but possibly promising. The post at the top of the list said, "driving from Portland to Seattle today can pick up anywhere along the way." I jotted down the phone number. A few posts below read "Watch out for the lunatic in the yellow honda!" A few posts below that one read "Beware the clown driving the blue bus tried to jump my bones!!" There weren't any other options for today. I typed the phone number for today's ride, pushed send. A few minutes later my phone lit up "Coming through Longview around 7:00 meet anywhere on i-5 -Ted"

"Count me in." I quickly sent back before I could think about it.

I pulled up Google Maps, clicked 'get directions'. It was 6.9 miles northeast from where I sat. I glanced at the clock, it read 5:30. I had an hour and a half to push nearly 7 miles to the i-5. I heaved my pack on my back, filled my water bottle at the water fountain on my way out. A wave of heat gushed over me as I walked out into the front lawn. I set a heading northeast and blazed through the humid haze with everything I had. Wilson would have been *pissed*.

I was able to stay back in a quiet neighborhood for awhile but then was forced to walk east on the sidewalk of a very busy street. Businesses lined either side and there were two lanes running in each direction, a median separating them. I walked down the narrow sidewalk on the southside. As fast as I possibly could considering the steam room of a night, the 70 pound pack on my back and the fact that my heart felt like it was going to explode. I battled onward for 25 minutes. I began to get dizzy. A pickup pulled into the quiet parking lot of the business ahead of me. The passenger side window rolled down and a woman in her 20's with a golden smile said, "You look like you're losing the battle to the heat, wanna ride?" "Yes I would." I said. The driver was a friendly looking guy about the same age as the woman. I threw my pack in the back and squeezed in the cab as the woman scooted over to make room. "I'm Josh, this is my girl Meg."

"Jack, nice to meet you."

"Where you headed?"

"I'm trying to get to the i-5, supposed to meet a guy who is hopefully going to give me a ride to Seattle."

"No problem, it's just a few miles down the road here. Would have been midnight before you made it on foot."

Josh and Meg were as nice as they come. They had recently returned home from a cross-country journey of their own and had fresh memories of life on the road. We soon pulled into a gas station, just off the i-5, into a parking spot in the shade of maple trees.

"Is your ride here?" asked Meg.

"I'm not sure, never met him."

Meg and Josh both looked confused.

"*Craigslist rideshare.*"

"Is that safe?" asked Josh.

"No."

"We thought about using it when we were on the road but heard some scary stories."

"My last ride was arrested mid-ride."

"Whoa."

"Yes."

I sent a text message to Ted indicating which gas station I was waiting at. "I used to vet my rides a bit before taking the ride, but lately I've just been getting in with whoever shows up."

I had 45 minutes to burn before 'Ted' was supposed to show up. I made my way towards a restaurant across the street from the gas station. I walked in and was pleasantly surprised to find out it was a taco joint. I ordered up 2 beef enchiladas and 2 beef tacos, leisurely finished my meal sipping on an ice water, watching the gas station parking lot out the window, not sure what I was looking for.

As I was making my way back across the street, I noticed a gold Honda peeling around the corner a block away, blasting toward the gas station like it was the final stretch. It screeched to a stop at the pumps. Before my phone even lit up I knew it was Ted. This Honda was gold, the one the *craigslist* post indicated was dangerous was yellow. Wasn't it?

A college aged kid emerged from the driver's side door. He was dressed in what looked to me like fire fighters gear, minus the helmet and overcoat. He was already pumping gas as I approached the car. "Ted?" He whirled around and flashed me a big snaggletooth smile. "Ted Taber that's me." He had a long skinny face with a birds-nest of brown hair mounted on top. His face and hands where smeared with black soot. He looked fairly harmless at first sight. I extended my hand across the top of the car. "Jack" good to meet you Taber. I put 40$ in his hand as he shook it, his smile got even bigger.

Ted was a wilderness firefighter in the heart of the fire season. He was coming from deep in the forest of eastern Oregon. He had been back in the bush for the last 45 days battling the flames on the front lines. He had the next 7 days off so he was heading home to Seattle to 'recoup'.

After filling gas we crawled into the beat up Honda and exited the gas station. Instead of merging back towards the interstate, Ted hung a right towards a strip mall. "Jackpot" he said quietly as we pulled into a parking spot directly in front of a weed dispensary. "Ran out of green a week ago back in the woods, time to go *all the way up*."

Inside Ted had quickly selected several grams of various exotically named strains, and was now torn between the pancake size weed infused chocolate cookie or the foot tall statuette of the 'Jolly Green Giant' that, according to the girl working, had enough *THC* in one of his boots to get 'half of Washington high'. "Jolly G." said Ted confidently.

Back on the road we began hot-boxing the Honda, alternating packing my bowl. After 5 bowls we took a breather. I became entranced in the scenery out the window for 10-15 minutes and when I 'came to' I noticed 'Jolly' sitting on the dash with his head, a portion of his torso, one boot, and both arms missing. Ted had both hands on the wheel, with his chin resting on the top. He was drooling. The expression on his face was akin to Tiger's mugshot. Cars were flying by us on all sides. I leaned over to check the speedometer, it read 40 mph. In an 80.

"You ok Ted?"

"Which oooooone?"

"Which what?"

"Foooooork"

"What fork?"

"In rooooooad" Ted said, squinting his eyes.

I looked down the interstate, it was straight as far as I could see.

"You want me to drive for a bit there Ted?"

"Where are we gooooiiinnnggg?"

"Just pull over here Ted, I'll take the wheel."

Ted drove the Honda partially into the long ditch grass, stopped. He opened the door and rolled out, crawled to the back door on all fours and struggled helplessly to open it. I helped him open the door, then I hopped in the driver's seat, Ted crawled into the back amid his firefighting gear.

"You ok buddy?"

"Joooolllllyyy G."

The Honda lurched forward as I let out the clutch and soon we were back amid the 5 lane traffic rolling north at, or near, the speed limit. I checked the rear-view mirror, Ted was kicking his legs out as if he was riding an air bike. I found jazz on a local station and soon fell into a road trance. I noticed a sign, Seattle was 45 miles away. I decided to call Dave, a friend from Bozeman that had moved to Seattle a few years back. Ted was making strange gurgling noises in the back seat, then started snoring loudly. I was able to reach Dave on the first try. He gave me directions to his place in Issaquah.

Seattle

W e blazed north into the outskirts of Seattle just as twilight was settling in. Orange, red light sparkled on the sides of the downtown buildings. To the west, from the fog of Puget Sound rose the Olympic mountains, their peaks white against the bonfire-colored sky. In the distance to the east loomed the slopes of Mt. Rainier. I was glad it was clear enough to get a good view, as I had heard that was rare.

I pulled the Honda in front of Dave's around 9:45pm. He was waiting on the sidewalk outside his condo with a big smile. I hadn't heard anything out of Ted for awhile, so I opened the back door to make sure he still had a pulse. He looked like he was in a coma but I did feel a pulse.

"McMurphy you crazy bastard! What's wrong with him?" asked Dave.

"Ahhhh, he ate enough THC to get the entire *state* high a few hours back."

"I would expect nothing less than for you to appear out of the ether in a Honda from last century with a quasi-firefighter in a weed-coma in the back seat." Dave said with a laugh.

"It's been wild."

"Come on in buddy."

I grabbed my pack from the trunk of the Honda, we made our way into the condo. Dave had a very nice place, he showed me to the guest bedroom upstairs and a bed had never looked so good. I hopped through the shower as it had been awhile, and then we walked down a few blocks to a neighborhood bar for dinner. It was nice getting caught up with Dave. He was an engineer at Boeing now, was dating a nice girl, and seemed to be enjoying life in Seattle. He told me about a winter camping trip on Rainier. I told him a few of the best tales from the road, he got a real kick out of them.

"So what's next?"

"I haven't gotten that far yet but I'm sure it will hit me in the next couple days if I get high enough."

"Well you're welcome here as long as you want, I'll be working long hours but the place is yours."

There was still no movement from Ted in the back seat of the Honda when we got back from dinner but I could feel breath when I put my hand in front of his mouth which was a good sign.

That night might very well be the best night of sleep of my life. I was out for a good 12 hours and awoke feeling ten years younger. In the morning I walked down the block to a coffee shop I had seen the night before on our walk back from dinner. The rich aroma of freshly brewed coffee hit me as I walked through the front door. I bought a light roast to go with a bagel, muffin, and 3 chocolate chip cookies. Breakfast.

It was a cool, cloudy morning in Seattle which felt glorious compared to the suffocating heat that had been the norm further south. Issaquah was beautiful, nestled into the hills around the city. Dave had said right out the back door was a great hike into the Issaquah Alps that led up to a perch with a stunning view of Seattle. I strolled down the sidewalk, back towards the condo, passing several people out for their morning dog-walk. As I approached the condo, I noticed a tow-truck loading Ted's car up. I hurried down the sidewalk but I was too late, arriving just as Ted was pulled away, apparently still comatose in the back seat. I noticed a sign that it was a no parking zone from 8-5 weekdays.

I rolled up 10 joints as I drank coffee to prepare for my hike, then lounged on Dave's back patio as I ate cookies and smoked 3 of the 10 in rapid succession. I could see the quiet hiking trail leading up through the thick rain-forest out back across the lawn. I packed water along with the baked goods I hadn't been able to finish. I took the hike slowly, my heart felt much better down here at sea level but Wilson still would not have approved. At the summit I found a bench overlooking the city. The clouds were low and soggy, I intermittently got glimpses of the towers downtown. It was quiet in the Alps today. I hadn't passed anyone on the trail, up top there was one woman doing yoga in the wet grass among the bushes on the far side, otherwise I had the hilltop to myself. I thought about Ron still out on the trail. I thought about Mia, wondering if she was still out there, if she was ok. I pulled out my tin of pre-rolls and fired one up. I selected an old jazz album on my ipod, pushed play, faded into a state of euphoria, sipping coffee from my thermos as I lit joint after joint puffing myself into complete oblivion.

I woke up on the bench, checked the time. It was 2:30. I fired up a joint.

I wandered around the Alps for a couple more hours and made it back to the condo around 4:30. I pulled a book off Dave's bookshelf and read a Paul Auster novel about life from the perspective of a dog. Dave made it back from work around 7, we decided to head downtown for dinner. We found a burger joint right on the water, near the ferris wheel, overlooking the harbor. All you can eat milkshakes. The snow-capped Olympics glowed in the orange dusk. The smell of the sea was strong on the wind.

The next two days I spent puffing joints like a chimney as I hiked in the Alps and contemplated my next move. I had briefly checked the Seattle *craigslist rideshare* page. The available rides essentially looked like signing up to be slaughtered. No, I was done with the road. I had my sight set squarely on the rails for my push east. Cargo train rail riding was something I'd wanted to try for years. I researched where the rail-yards were located in Seattle and decided I would launch the torpedo east the following evening at dark. *Fuck it.*

Into the Cascades

As the last of the crimson twilight faded into the Olympics, Dave turned onto 4th ave S, which ran along the west side of the Union Pacific rail yard, just northwest of Beacon Hill. It had rained steadily throughout the day, leaving everything shiny, wet. The rich smell of rain and wet stone rode the cool breeze. Before long, we spotted a pocket of tree's and greenery, I said, "this is the spot." Dave slowed, pulled over to the side of the road. He looked scared.

"Call if shit hits the fan."

"This time tomorrow, or maybe the next day, I'll be sitting atop Peet's hill watching the sun set behind the Tobacco Roots... or I'll be a memory." I said with a smile but Dave didn't laugh. "It was good to see you bud, thanks again." I waved him off down the wet blacktop and then turned to face the circus of steel.

It was a true *cluster-fuck* of trains, steel, sparks, workers loading and unloading, repairing the giant rolling boxes of metal. I was wearing the darkest colors I had, my waterproof hiking boots, and had a few black garbage bags along to hopefully camouflage myself as a pile of garbage. I nestled into the dark pocket of trees and shrubs laying as low as I could. The previous day, I had taken an underground internet forum crash course in 'riding the rails'. But apparently it was not far enough underground to give away any 'useful information' as was clearly stated at the top of the forum. The main thing I had learned was rail riding was a highly guarded 'lifestyle' shrouded in mystery and no authentic 'rider of the rails' would divulge much information about how to actually ride the rails. Essentially, to be an authentic rail rider you had to jump in the deep end, learn how to swim. Over 50 percent of 'attempties', mostly 'weekend warrior rail riders' (blow-pop wielding thrill seekers! hacks!)(according to one forum contributor) shortly after jumping into said 'deep end' learned they could not in fact 'swim' (quite possibly due to a lack of information.) I had pushed up my trip by a day to avoid a Saturday departure, between that and the garbage bags, maybe the other hobos would assume I was the 'real deal'.

I would have thought the billy club yielding masses of meat eager to club any living man or beast into complete submission that would even *think* about riding a train, would have been enough of a deterrent to keep rail riding numbers 'in check'. My research had indicated these 'bulls' would rip around the rail yards on A.T.V's, golf carts, even diesel pickups looking for hobo's to take out their frustration, on. Which was apparently a lot by the looks of some of the photos of hobo's beat to a bloody pulp posted on the forums. This was the one thing I was prepared for. I had stopped at the outdoor store near Dave's in Issaquah and picked up 2 fresh cans of bear spray to go with supplies to fashion a double holster belt, which also had a spot for my bear spray goggles so I could 'spray at will'.

The patch of trees I was hiding in had remnants of a hobo camp, or *jungle*. A soggy bag of rice. Cigarette butts littered the muddy ground, dried out orange peels were scattered around with tattered pieces of clothing and an old heavily chewed dog bone. I was in the right spot. As far as how to know which train was going where you wanted to go, some may say otherwise, but the truth is it came down to essentially dumb luck. There were charts, maps, schedule's, hidden and coded out there somewhere in cyber-land and beyond but with constantly changing conditions the accuracy was *shoddy* at best. Your options were basically to summon the balls to walk up to a rail yard worker in the departure section of the yard, who looked like he didn't give a fuck about his job and simply ask, hoping they knew what they were talking about....or just wait for a train that was moving through the yard at 8 mph or less, make a run for it, avoid the bulls, hop on, and hope it's destination was in the direction you wanted to go. And three points of contact at all times!! That piece of information was readily divulged on the forum, whatever you do while riding a train you must must must maintain three points of contact!

I sat hunched in the bushes with a garbage bag over me for cover, watching the *cluster-fuck* of moving steel going about its nightly business in the yard. After studying the mess for several hours, I had located the departure section of the yard. Yard workers readied train cars for *'final departure'*. Bulls roamed like caged tigers. I had seen one train come lumbering through the yard without stopping which told me that line was the *'main line'*. That's the line I wanted. When a train came rolling through, rolling north on the main-line at a pace slow enough for me to hop on, and the coast was clear as far as bulls, that was my 'window of opportunity' (and what an opportunity it was). Another few hours passed, it was now 1 in the morning. It rained on and off and despite my garbage bag I was beginning to get saturated by the cold pounding rain. One train came rolling in on the main-line, but it came screeching, steaming to a stop when it made it into the yard and a maintenance crew began working on the engine. I smoked a joint under the shelter of my bag and somehow dozed off laying on my pack in the mud. I still hadn't seen a fellow hobo waiting out here in the lurches beyond the yard. I didn't know if that was good or bad. I awoke soaked and shivering around 3:30 am, decided I was going for the next train to come rolling in on the main-line. *Fuck it*. I would only have the cover of darkness for a few more hours, and I considered the rain an ally in deterring capture by the bulls, why I wasn't sure.

Around 4:15 a Union Pacific engine came chugging into the yard. I put on my makeshift bear spray goggles, stood from the swamp, began running hunched over towards the yard. I noticed movement to my left and right. To the left, there were at least 4 hobos that had emerged from a jungle to the north hobbling/running towards the train. To my right, 3 more hobos were running in the same direction. I was in the *great war*, a platoon of highly intoxicated hobo doughboys were charging the line! I decided it was a good sign that this seemed to be a popular train. I was hoping these blitzed vagrants knew something I didn't. We made it halfway across no mans land when I spotted the first set of bulls come ripping down the gravel road along the main-line in a golf cart. I got both hands on my bear-spray, continued the charge. The pumping adrenaline had slowed everything down, it seemed as if time was moving in slow motion. Out of my peripheral vision it appeared the hobo to my immediate left was twirling nunchucks. *How high was I?* The hobos on the eastern flank were drunk as loons, laughing hysterically as they stumbled through the endless sets of tracks that is 'no mans land', on toward enemy lines. Speaking of bulls,

another set of them had ripped around the corner on foot,
running along with the train, armed with various weapons
around their belts.

The train was a *beauty*. Mostly grain hoppers with
porches and petroleum tankers, with a few suicide cars
mingled in. It was moving pretty good, catch-able, but by
no means a 'gimmie'. The hobo twirling nunchucks was the
first to make contact with a bull. He was immediately lit
up like a Christmas tree by a taser. He crumpled into a
sizzling heap, his nunchucks clinking and clanking sadly to
the ground. Then they started in on him with billy-clubs. I
reached down into my holsters, grabbed my cans and let 'er
rip right into the faces of the bulls on my way by.
Thankfully the hobo was being beaten face down, out of
harms way. Both bulls went down to the ground squirming
and flopping around like fish out of water. I was running
full tilt now, eyes set squarely on the porch of a grainer
rolling north 100 ft ahead. I put the jets on and ran faster
than I had since the Yosemite 'incident', my heart was
beating harder than a pow wow drum beat. The two bulls
on foot had gone after the drunk hobos on the eastern flank,
I looked back, they were beating them like *pinatas*. The
casualties of war. It was a clear path to the grainer
(apparently, the Rolls Royce of cargo train cars), still 50 ft
to the south of me and I would beat it to the tracks in front
of me. I reached the dirt road that runs parallel with the
train and began running north along with the train, looking
over my right shoulder like a wide receiver looking back
for the long ball. The grainer fell directly into my path and
I had a clean hop up onto the back ladder. I looked out
over the battle field, it was a sad sight. The poor drunk
fellows on the southern flank were getting absolutely
marinated by the bulls on foot. The hobo who had been
tased was laying motionless, face down in mud. The bulls I
had sprayed were stumbling around like angry bumble bees
with blindfolds on. 2/3 of the northern flank were in hot
pursuit of grainers on up ahead, running alongside the train

like their lives depended on it (they quite possibly did).
The first one had a clean hop onto the back ladder, but the
other guy who had 8-10 gallon jugs of water crudely tied
and tangled onto his pack and person was huffing, puffing,
running as fast as his short stubby legs could carry him but
it was just too much weight, he was beginning to lose
ground. Just when it looked like he had no chance, he
made a diving lunge toward the back railing of the passing
car and somehow his hands found iron and clamped on like
hawk talons around the gills of a fish. His feet and legs
were now dragging behind him, beside the train, far too
close for comfort to the wheels. His friend was two cars in
front of him and had no real way of helping. Water
splashed and sloshed everywhere as lids were popped off,
jugs bouncing along the ground. Just when it looked like
he couldn't possibly hold on any longer, the third member
of the norther flank appeared from thin air atop of the car
he was dragging from. He shimmied off the roof onto the
back porch, grabbed the dragging hobo by the forearms and
somehow hauled the bowling ball of a man and all 8-10
sloshing water bottles back up onto the porch. He then
quickly shimmied back atop of the rail-car, disappearing
over the far side.

"You Ok over there buddy?" I yelled to the
bowling ball.

"Lost some water."

"You almost lost your legs!"

"I've dragged many a mile behind trains in my day
boy!"

"Glad you're alright man!"

We blazed north on the *high-line* winding through
Seattle proper, the suburbs, into the towering Cascades to
the east, the faint outline of the jagged peaks against the
dark sky. The train quickly picked up speed once we were
out of the city. A long sad train horn floated over the
lonely countryside. The icy breeze chilled my wet clothes
to the bone. The air was damp, misty, but the rain had

stopped for now. I set up camp on the porch of my grainer, tying my garbage bags to the railing of the porch as a makeshift wind block. I fastened my pack to the railing with a carabiner. I sipped at my 3 liter pouch of water, the ice-cold water chilled me further. I carefully got my sleeping bag off my pack and out of its bag. I immediately tied it off to my jacket in case the wind tried to steal it. I managed to get into my bag and when I lay my pack down, the bottom, full of sweatshirts, made for a descent pillow. I was actually pretty damn comfortable, all things considered. Now, to get *high*. I found my bowl in a jacket pocket, it was pre-packed. I ducked my head down into my jacket out of the wind, sparked up the bowl, hot-boxing my coat. I lay down on my porch, looking up, diamonds strewn across black velvet, the stars ran burning down the sky. Lulled into a trance by the hypnotic clickity clack of the track. I dozed off and on and then was awoken by the booming voice of the bowling ball up two cars ahead.

"Ok I think we're fixin' to go into the tunnel! Yep heerrreee we goooooo! Come on!"

I sat up on my porch, the cold wind snapped me awake. I looked on up ahead and in the dim morning light I could see the entrance of a dark tunnel a quarter mile up ahead on the tracks. *Fuck me.*

"We could be in there 20 minutes! Locked into that carbon monoxide! Or if he stops in the middle like at Tennessee pass. And then guns it. There's smoke everywhere!! But anyway..." The bowling ball yelled maniacally. "This whole entire train is about 130 cars and it's about 50 percent lpd liquified petroleum gas loaded cars!...So if you hear of a train derailment in western Washington with a massive explosion you'll know it's this one!!...Stuff like that don't scare me! If you're going to be in a derail you're not going to live through it anyway so you might as well be cremated at the same time! Save your family money!" yelled the bowling ball, over the wind, in a thick West Virginia accent. "I broke the tip off my dang gone knife! Now if I run into any trouble I'm going to have to stab someone extra hard to get it to go in!!"

The bowling ball was clearly a rail-riding veteran.

"You can't ride them, well you can it's called riding suicide I've done it before matter fact I did it on a COAL CAR, just sit somewhere where it's flat and try not to go to SLEEEEP!!"

The dark archway loomed up ahead. Closer, closer. I hadn't read anything about tunnels on the forum, but I did remember hearing somewhere that the buildup of carbon monoxide in these tunnels could be deadly. I read the sign on the top of the entrance to the tunnel. "Cascade tunnel 7.8 miles long completed 1929" Under the original sign was posted: Fans not working: USE RESPIRATORS!

We entered the tunnel doing at least 50 mph, there was no time or way to get off. And then we were engulfed by the blackness. The air was musty, dank, rich with the smell of railroad ties and diesel exhaust. I pulled my shirt up over my face, tried to remain calm. I watched as the arch of light became smaller and smaller behind us, the thimble of light soon snuffed out by darkness. The train rumbled on relentlessly deeper, deeper into the mountain. It didn't take long before I couldn't get an adequate breath. I knew my shirt was useless filtering carbon monoxide. It was just a matter of time now. I tried to pull in breaths of air but my lungs seemed to contract and seize up, not letting me get the satisfaction of oxygen into my body. Soon, the dizziness kicked in and I clasped my fingers through the holes in the grate floor of the porch.

"COME ON! LET'S GET OUT OF THIS DAMN HOLE! I'M SUFFOCATING IN HERE!" I heard the bowling ball yell desperately over the deafening rumble of the train.

My heart started to pound furiously, my arms and legs became heavy, my vision blurred. Was this it? *The end!* I thought about how damn rich and vibrant life had been. How at times along the way *I had lived the lively fuck out of life.* I thought about how the pain would *finally* be gone. *I was ready for that.* My eye's closed, I faded deep into my own consciousness. The light of eternity, gardens of paradise. I felt myself topple onto my side, my chest barely moving now. A calming weakness washed over my body. I let go. A piercing arch shaped keyhole ribbon of light illuminated the beginning on the foggy horizon.

Made in the USA
Middletown, DE
09 January 2022

58255899R00096